FOREVER HER MARQUESS

DUKES MOST WANTED
BOOK TWO

SCARLETT SCOTT

Forever Her Marquess

Dukes Most Wanted Book Two

All rights reserved.

Copyright © 2024 by Scarlett Scott

Published by Happily Ever After Books, LLC

Edited by Grace Bradley and Lisa Hollett, Silently Correcting Your Grammar

Cover Design by Wicked Smart Designs

This book or any portion thereof may not be reproduced or used in any manner whatsoever without the express written permission of the publisher except for the use of brief quotations in a book review.

The unauthorized reproduction or distribution of this copyrighted work is illegal. No part of this book may be scanned, uploaded, or distributed via the Internet or any other means, electronic or print, without the publisher's permission. Criminal copyright infringement, including infringement without monetary gain, is punishable by law.

This book is a work of fiction and any resemblance to persons, living or dead, or places, events, or locales, is purely coincidental. The characters are productions of the author's imagination and used fictitiously.

For more information, contact author Scarlett Scott.

https://scarlettscottauthor.com

For all the readers who have been asking for Clementine and Dorset's happily ever after. They're finally where they've always belonged.

CHAPTER 1

She was in the wrong bedroom.

Clementine realized her error the moment she swept into the chamber, breathless and abuzz with anticipation of the prank she intended to play on her friend Lady Charity Manners. It was the scent that alerted her first.

Musky and manly with a decisive edge of citrus and a note of something richer. It was an enticing scent, she couldn't lie. The sort of scent that made her wonder to whom it belonged.

And then it was the personal items neatly laid out on a nearby dresser, including a leather case that had been left open to reveal a brush, a razor, and a small tin of shaving soap. Beside that, a box of cigars and some matches. These were the trappings of men and most certainly not the delicate, elegant brushes and pots to be expected in the toilette of a lady.

"Oh dear," she muttered to herself.

She had, quite clearly, managed to land herself in a gentleman's chamber. And the footsteps beyond in the hall, coupled with the deep, masculine voices, told her that it was entirely possible the gentleman in question was about to return.

Frantically, Clementine searched for a means of escape as the voices in the hall came nearer. But there was no other means of exit, save the door she had just entered.

As a self-professed matchmaker, Clementine knew better than anyone just how damning it could be to find oneself unexpectedly alone in the wrong room with someone. Particularly when she had no notion of who that someone was.

Where could she go? How could she hide? A glance at the imposing high tester nestled against the far wall proved hiding beneath it an unreliable option. She would never manage to squeeze herself, bustle and all, under the frame. Her gaze lit on the voluminous curtains bracketing the window that overlooked the Sherborne Manor park.

Perhaps she could hide herself behind one half of the drapery.

Frantic, she hastened across the Axminster before sliding behind the curtain. She scarcely had a moment to arrange the window dressing around her and attempt to flatten her skirts before the door to the bedroom swung open.

"...a game of billiards later, old chap."

Her breath caught in her throat at the voice, for she knew exactly to whom it belonged.

And the Marquess of Dorset despised her.

The feeling was mutual.

It all stemmed, she suspected, from her matchmaking attempts between Lady Anna Harcastle and the Marquess of Huntly. Attempts which had proven successful when Lady Anna and Huntly had fallen desperately in love and married.

She closed her eyes tightly, wondering why, of all the rooms she might have inadvertently entered by mistake, she should have found *his*.

Because that was the rotten nature of the luck she had. Which was to say, she had none at all. It would have been a fate far better to have found herself accidentally inside Lady Featherstone's chamber, and the dowager marchioness was a vicious-tongued gossip everyone sought to avoid at all costs.

The click of the door closing was followed by footfalls on the carpet.

She held her breath.

"Since when do curtains have feet?" he drawled.

Oh, blast. Her heart plummeted. The dratted window covering wasn't long enough, and he had spied her. Perhaps if she said nothing, he would be a gentleman, understand she'd entered the wrong room, and go away so that she might escape in peace.

Any hope of that was dashed when the curtain was whisked aside, and she was presented with the sight of the Marquess of Dorset hovering over her, too tall and irritatingly handsome, his vibrant, green eyes narrowing when he recognized her.

"You," he growled, his lip curling into a sneer.

"My lord—" she began, only to be interrupted.

"What the devil are you doing in my room, Lady Clementine?" the marquess demanded.

She cleared her throat, giving him her most winning smile in the hope it might dim some of his ire. "I have a perfectly good explanation."

His jaw tensed. "If you're intending to cause more trouble, be warned, madam. I'll not suffer your machinations."

His disdain for her was palpable. He had made his dislike for her known on several occasions at Society events. However, he had never been so brutally earnest.

"I was seeking Lady Charity's chamber," she explained. "I intended to give her a fright when she entered. However, I must have made a mistake, because this is not her room."

"It is mine."

"I can see that now," she said weakly, keenly aware of the window at her back and his big body between herself and the door. "I apologize for the inconvenience."

"You expect me to believe you innocently wandered into the wrong room?"

"Yes."

"*You?* The lady notorious for all her matchmaking escapades, for catching couples in compromising positions, had no notion of which room she was entering?"

She smiled encouragingly. "Yes."

"Ha!" He barked out a vicious, bitter burst of laughter so sudden and loud it caused her to flinch. "You must think me the world's greatest idiot."

Her mouth moved, unable to form sentences for a moment. In truth, she did think him an idiot, but for a different reason entirely.

"Perhaps not the world's greatest," she allowed, unable to hold her tongue.

The Marquess of Dorset simply had that effect upon her. He was a bitter rake who was handsome and knew it too well. Who had left a trail of broken hearts in his dazzlingly elegant wake. He was the sort of man a lady of intellect never dared trust.

"Do you know what I ought to do, Lady Clementine?" he asked, stroking his jaw idly, as if he had all the time in the world to corner her here against the window of his bedroom.

"Yes," she said tartly. "You ought to step aside so that I may go."

"Not yet, I don't think," Dorset said smoothly.

She considered a means of escape, but he was standing so close, and she feared that movement in any direction would lead to either her bringing down the drapes or brushing against him.

"Dorset," she protested pointedly. "Surely you realize that my lingering here is a risk neither of us should dare to take."

"Hmm," was all he said, a troubling glint entering his eye. "Why not, Lady Clementine?"

"You know precisely why."

"What if I don't? Explain it to me, if you please."

Her panic was rising. The longer she remained trapped in his room with him, the greater the danger of discovery.

She took a step to the right, her bustle brushing along the windowpane and catching on something. Dorset took a step as well, his countenance bordering on fiendish.

He was enjoying her entrapment, she realized. Enjoying her discomfiture.

"My lord," she tried again, seeking mercy and reason, two traits which he apparently lacked.

Dorset smiled, and she couldn't deny the effect it had on her. "Enlighten me. I'll wait."

Her cheeks were annoyingly hot. If she'd been carrying a fan, she would have put it to excellent use. And perhaps also used it to poke him soundly in the eye.

"If I am seen leaving your room by any of our fellow guests, scandal will be unavoidable," she gritted through clenched teeth. "I haven't come to this house party to set tongues wagging or find myself entrapped in a marriage of convenience."

"Do you imagine any of your past victims sought to be trapped?" he asked sharply.

Victims? Why, he made it sound as if she were a murderer stalking the streets in the darkest night, claiming souls.

"I haven't any victims," she countered coldly. "Now if you please, move so that I may pass and remove myself from this dreadful situation."

"Always interesting when the spider gets caught in her own web," he said.

And Clementine quite lost her patience.

"Blast it, Dorset," she blurted, "are you a madman?"

He gave her a speculative look. "In addition to being an idiot, you mean?"

He was *definitely* a madman.

Vivi had invited a lunatic to her country house party, and now Clementine was trapped with him.

She tried sweeping to the right, but her bustle remained caught. The sound of tearing echoed in the quiet of the room.

"Oh good heavens," she cried, truly in distress now, for she was wearing one of her favorite afternoon gowns, and there was only one thing worse than being discovered alone with the Marquess of Dorset in his bedroom, and that was being discovered alone with him whilst her gown bore a giant tear in the silk skirts.

Everyone would think something terribly unseemly had occurred.

"I do believe you've torn a hole in your gown," Dorset observed calmly. "You should have taken greater care."

"How was I to have taken greater care, you lummox?" Clementine pushed at his insufferably broad shoulders, but the bounder refused to budge. "This is all your fault. You entrapped me here and wouldn't allow me to go."

"You entrapped yourself, Lady Clementine." He frowned down at her, craning his neck, still unmoving, despite her efforts. "Turn, if you please. Allow me to see the damage done."

She didn't want him to inspect her ruined gown. Didn't want his assistance. Most assuredly didn't want his proximity. The scent she had detected upon first entering the bedroom was more pronounced now—coming from *him*. And it was disturbingly pleasant, despite the distinctly irritating source.

"Kindly move away so that I can see for myself," she ordered him.

He made a *tsk* sound, as if he were warning a naughty child. "Have you eyes in the back of your head?"

"No, but I've a neck that turns."

"I'm only trying to help you."

They glared at each other.

The sound of more voices in the hall reached her. Clementine huffed a sigh, surrendering.

"Very well," she muttered. "If you must."

She turned to the sound of more ripping silk.

"It would seem your gown is still stuck on the tieback," he said.

"Obviously," she ground out. "Why did you not tell me so before I turned?"

She knew the answer, of course. It was because he was a devious rogue.

He leaned nearer, the press of his large body against hers inevitable as he struggled to pull her silk from the gilt hook upon which it had been helplessly snagged. And curse him, but his nearness wasn't entirely despicable.

She was *moved*, something inside her tightening, growing acutely aware of him in a new and dangerous way.

Clementine held her breath and averted her gaze out the window. And that was when she saw the dragon marchioness, Lady Featherstone, walking on the path below with her daughter, Lady Edith. Clementine gasped, horror clawing at her. She could not afford to be seen in the Marquess of Dorset's bedroom window. Not by anyone, but most especially not by the dowager.

Mindlessly, she threw herself at the marquess.

There was another great rending of fabric, and then the two of them toppled as one to the Axminster.

CHAPTER 2

She was a bloody lunatic.

That was the sole explanation for Lady Clementine Hammond's presence in Ambrose's bedroom. For her hiding behind his curtains. For her every exasperating attempt at matchmaking that had come before, successful and otherwise. For all the lives she had damned well ruined with her nonsensical meddling.

Final, incontrovertible proof of her lunacy? The chit had tackled him.

Being the gentleman that he was, Ambrose had made certain to land first, gentling her fall.

But the process had knocked the wind from him. And she was currently smothering him with her breasts. Breasts which he could now attest to being delightfully bountiful. Much more than pert handfuls. Indeed, his face was drowning in bubbies.

As pleasant as he may have found such a position had the breasts smothering him belonged to anyone other than *her*, it was entirely lost on him now.

Well, almost entirely lost. His cock had other ideas. Stupid ideas.

Ideas his mind would never allow.

His hands found purchase on her waist, and he pulled her down his body, her curves molding to him in all the right places.

Her eyes were wide and startlingly blue as they met his. "What are you doing?"

Her daring would never cease to amaze him.

"I am lying on my back after having been leapt upon by a madwoman," he said, and not without irony.

"It is you who is mad," she snapped, still lying atop him. "Else you would have allowed me to leave your chamber following my embarrassing mistake. Instead, you held me prisoner."

By God.

"As I recall it, madam, the hook held you prisoner," he corrected her.

"It is your fault that I was in your window when Lady Featherstone was walking below it." She grasped his lapels, tugging. "She may have seen me. For all I know, she is currently gleefully carrying the tale of me in your private rooms to every other guest in attendance."

It would certainly serve Lady Clementine right if the dowager had indeed spied her. But Ambrose had no wish to be included in a scandal involving the meddlesome chit. Indeed, he had no wish to have anything to do with her at all.

Not entirely true, whispered a wicked little voice within. One he promptly silenced.

"You are the one who entered my bedroom uninvited," he pointed out, trying to be gallant and not notice the way her present position pushed Lady Clementine's breasts up in her corset so that they threatened to spill from her bodice.

And failing utterly.

Could he see the pink crests of her areolas? His mouth went dry.

"Unintentionally," she parried.

"You are the one who attempted to hide behind the curtain," he returned. "And poorly, I might add. Surely you must have realized that the window dressings don't go to the floor."

The chagrined expression on her countenance told him that she had not.

It might have been laughable. Perhaps, if she were any other woman, adorable, even.

But this was Lady Clementine Hammond, and nothing about her was either laughable or adorable. Deplorable might have been a more apt descriptor. Despite the undeniable allure of her décolletage.

"It seemed an excellent option at the time," she grumbled.

That was when Ambrose realized how good Lady Clementine's waist felt in his hands. And how her sweet floral scent wrapped around him like a loving caress. And just how very kissable her soft, pink pout was. She was strikingly lovely, and he had known it before, but somehow, it had been far easier to ignore when they'd been trading barbs and she'd not been a delectable weight atop him.

Fucking hell.

Had he hit his head when he had landed? That was the only excuse for such thoughts where she was concerned.

"One must wonder at your judgment," he said, but the words were meant for himself as much as for Lady Clementine.

Because he was still thinking terrible, disreputable thoughts about her. And his cock was twitching to attention.

"You loathe me," she said, surprising him, her brow furrowing.

Guilt lanced him. She seemed suddenly vulnerable, as

delicate as Sèvres. Not at all the hardened manipulator he had believed her to be, watching her maneuverings from afar.

"Loathe is rather a strong word," he said, flexing his fingers on her waist, liking the supple softness of her curves too much.

She needed to get off him.

Out of his room.

Well beyond his reach before he was tempted to do something truly reckless, like kiss her.

"Why do you dislike me so?" she asked, sounding a bit hurt.

And blast him, but the urge to reassure her, to soothe her worries, hit him strong and hard. Which made no sense, for the woman in his arms was responsible for the marriage he had needed slipping through his fingers like water. Lady Anna Harcastle's dowry had been precisely what he had required to help save his moldering ancestral estate from impending ruin. Instead, she had married Huntly, and Ambrose's debts—largely incurred by his wastrel brother, who'd saddled him with the burden after succumbing to a lung infection—had continued to mount.

But it wasn't just her dowry he'd needed, if he were honest. He'd respected the lady. Had grown quite fond of her. He didn't dare call it love now, though he'd been foolish enough to do so in the past.

"Do you think we might finish this conversation on our feet?" he asked Lady Clementine curtly, reminded of all the reasons he should not soften toward her.

For he'd been forced to attend this blasted house party in the hope of finding a marriageable lady. He couldn't lie. The American heiresses attending had proven an impressive lure. He hadn't known, however, that Lady Clementine would be in attendance as well.

"Yes, of course," she said, color tingeing her cheekbones as she struggled to remove herself from him.

The result of her graceless writhing and wiggling was his rapidly stiffening cock. His body liked Lady Clementine Hammond well enough, even if the rest of Ambrose did not.

"Let me help you," he ground out, desperate to keep her from noticing the effect she had on him through her petticoats and skirts.

"I don't need your aid."

He couldn't contain his amusement at her arch pronouncement. "The way you didn't need my assistance when you were caught on the hook?"

"You're insufferable," she said.

"You're meddlesome," he countered.

They stared at each other. And something shifted in the air between them, becoming heavy and hot as it burned to the surface. It was sizzling and sparking and wholly unavoidable. Attraction, he realized, like a jolt of pure electricity sent through his veins. He wanted to spar with her and kiss her breathless at the same time.

Her head dipped, her breath coasting over his lips in a tantalizing whisper. And he was still falling into her gaze, telling himself they weren't going to do this, they weren't going to kiss, and yet knowing it was inevitable that they did. His hand crept to her nape, slipping into her silken hair to cup the base of her head. Holding her there, not forcing. Gently. Delicately. Showing her what he wanted without saying the words.

And then her mouth was on his.

My God, was all he could think, astounded as his mind and body rejoiced as one.

Yes, indeed, her mouth was on his, firm and demanding, hot and decadent, and he forgot every reason he had for not liking her when her lips moved. She kissed the way he had imagined she would, with wild abandon. It was the kiss of a woman who was self-assured. The kiss of a woman who wandered into bedrooms and orchestrated matrimonial matches and did whatever she bloody well pleased.

It was the most passionate kiss he'd received from any lover in his life.

Which was wrong, all wrong, because this was the dreadful Lady Clementine, the matchmaker who had ruined his chances with Lady Anna, the woman whose every garish dress was adorned with flowers, as if she were a garden in full bloom. The woman who had snuck into his bedroom and then blamed him for her unwanted presence there.

And yet somehow, it was right, all right. *Too* right, except for her domination of the kiss. That wasn't right at all.

Ambrose rolled them as one until Lady Clementine was on her side instead of atop him and he could devour her mouth as he wanted, taking control of the kiss. Her lips were soft, so soft, and full. Tempting. Delicious. Lips he never wanted to stop kissing.

What was the matter with him? She had ensorcelled him. That was surely the answer. He'd struck his head, and then the devious chit had cast some manner of spell.

But oh, what a seductive spell it was. Her luscious curves pressed into him, her arms wrapped around his neck, and she opened with a husky sort of sound hatched from deep in her throat. A sound that was invitation and surrender in one. He dipped his tongue inside to taste Madeira cake laced with tea. She needed no coaxing, responding in kind as the kiss deepened, turning carnal and hungry.

Desire snaked down his spine in a sinuous rush. His cock was rigid in his trousers, and every part of him was roaring with the need to do more than kiss this woman.

An impossibility, of course.

The woman was Lady Clementine Hammond.

An innocent.

He tore his mouth from hers, his breathing uneven. Her eyes were glazed with passion, her thick lashes low, lips parted and swollen from their kisses.

"You…kissed me," she murmured.

And he was not at all surprised that she had once again uttered something so thoroughly wrongheaded. She was, in fact, the one who had initiated their reckless embrace. Who had fallen atop him and then smothered his mouth with her own lush lips. They were, even now, lying on their sides like lovers entwined, as if they were reluctant to let the other go.

"You kissed me first," he pointed out wryly. "And you liked it."

"I didn't," she denied, her tone one of prim affront.

He couldn't contain his grin. She was a ridiculous woman. A ridiculous, maddening, beautiful, tempting woman. Perversely, he wanted more.

"Then prove it," he dared. "Kiss me again."

She tugged him to her, her eager lips opening over his. He was lost again, caught up in the moment, in her. He gave her his tongue, and she moaned approvingly. His hands traveled with a mind of their own, spurred by the need to feel the womanly curves hidden within her silk and petticoats. But he was thwarted by undergarments and reminded at the twinge in his left hip that they were lying on the floor.

Reality collided with desire.

This had progressed beyond madness to sheer stupidity.

Why, it was entirely possible that Lady Clementine had planned this tableau. That she had wandered into his bedroom with the intention of entrapping him and had then done her utmost to seduce him. And if so, she had certainly succeeded. His hand had been itching to glide beneath her skirts. A few more kisses, and he might have allowed himself the liberty.

He tore his lips from hers, panting, staring at her, searching for any hints of scheming. But Lady Clementine's ordinarily haughty demeanor had gone lush and almost dreamy. Her kiss-stung lips were parted. She looked, in a word, dazed.

As dazed as he felt. He liked this look on her, so much less cunning and calculated. So much softer.

Ambrose swallowed hard against a rush of emotion he had no business feeling where she was concerned. "I believe you've proven my point, Lady Clementine."

She blinked, her body stiffening in his arms, as if the spell had been broken. "Good heavens. I have no notion of what came over me. I must go. I should never have… I don't even *like* you."

Lady Clementine spoke so swiftly, her words tripping over themselves in her eagerness to speak them. Horror dawned on her countenance as she struggled into a sitting position, no doubt weighed down by her lavishly bedecked gown, bustle, and underskirts. Grimly, Ambrose helped her before rising to his feet and offering her a hand.

"The feeling is mutual, my lady."

She ignored his hand, scrambling to her feet herself. Of course she did. Somehow, her stubborn nature and the fact that she was responsible for his lack of a wife and much-needed funds didn't keep him from wanting to kiss her again. From longing to sweep her into his arms and carry her to the bed across the room.

Lady Clementine shook out her skirts, holding herself with a regal air that belied her recent presence on the floor with him, kissing him witless. "Pray keep this unfortunate incident between the two of us, Lord Dorset."

She wanted to keep it a secret? Fine, then. Perhaps she hadn't orchestrated this contretemps with the intention of trapping him into matrimony.

"I wouldn't dream of telling a soul," he assured her sharply. "This was an unfortunate aberration."

"Most unfortunate," she agreed coolly, a decided pinch at the corners of her lips giving away her displeasure.

"We are agreed, then." He plucked at the sleeves of his coat, averting his gaze from the sight of her, so gloriously mussed and obviously kissed. It was becoming rapidly apparent that Lady Clementine Hammond was his own personal Gorgon. Only, there was a single portion of anatomy that turned to stone when he looked upon her. "What happened here goes no further than the two of us, and it won't happen again."

She scoffed, as if the very notion of kissing him in the future were preposterous. "Naturally not."

"Excellent," he bit out, trying not to snarl, irked in spite of himself by her icy rejection. "You should go."

"Nothing would please me more," she said.

He tugged at his right sleeve a final time, then brushed away a speck of lint. "You should take care next time you wander into a bedroom uninvited, Lady Clementine."

"I can assure you I'll take every care in the future."

Ambrose glanced up at her, because he couldn't not, blast the woman. And she was still looking every bit as thoroughly ravished as she had moments before. The urge to undo some of her buttons, to set his mouth upon the smooth column of her throat and taste her skin, was sudden and feverish.

He needed a drink.

"Good," he gritted. "Now, if you don't mind, *exeunt* stage left."

"Thrilled to," she offered with a tight smile, before whisking away in a swirl of ridiculously bright skirts and silk flowers.

Ambrose watched her hips sway as she bustled across the Axminster before opening the door a crack to peer into the hallway. The moment was not unlike many a country house party scene, with a pair of lovers hoping to avoid scrutiny or detection. However, Lady Clementine was not his lover, and if someone discovered her leaving his chamber, he was going to have to marry her.

And marrying the calculating chit who had stolen his chance at restoring his depleted coffers was out of the question. He wouldn't wed her if she were the last woman in England.

Even if he liked kissing her far more than he ought to.

Without offering him a backward glance, she slipped from his chamber into the hall beyond, the door closing softly behind her. He held his breath, listening for voices, any hint she had been spotted leaving the wrong room. But after a few moments had passed, he exhaled, relief washing over him.

Disaster had been narrowly avoided.

CHAPTER 3

"You just barely avoided utter disaster and ruination," Charity told Clementine, sounding part intrigued, part disappointed.

No one adored gossip more than Lady Charity Manners—only when she wasn't the cause of it, that was. And no one knew better than Clementine just how close she had come to being ruined. Completely.

Indeed, if the Marquess of Dorset hadn't stopped kissing her when he had…

No, she wouldn't finish that thought, for it didn't bear contemplation. He *had* stopped kissing her, and she *had* regained her wits, and she had all but run from his chamber, never to return.

She fluttered her fan, attempting to cool her heated cheeks, which she attributed solely to the summer weather and not at all to the troubling reminiscences of Dorset's mouth on hers. "Trust me, I know."

"Are you overheated?" Vivi, the Duchess of Bradford, Clementine's hostess and dear friend, asked solicitously.

Blast. She was overwrought. And it was unseasonably

warm for Yorkshire at this time of year. Yes, that was all it was.

She smiled at her friend, fanning herself more vigorously. "I'm perfectly well."

"You look flushed, Tiny," Charity observed, using the diminutive she had settled upon for Clementine during their finishing school days.

She clenched her jaw so hard that her teeth ached. "You know I hate it when you call me that, Charity. And it's exceedingly warm outside. Of course I'm flushed."

Indeed, despite forgoing her drawers as Charity swore by doing in the summer months, Clementine was sweltering. The three of them were walking together to the Sherborne Manor gardens, where Vivi had arranged an elaborate game of life-size lawn chess for her guests. Clementine was already regretting her decision to confide in her friends. But she had needed to tell someone what had occurred in Dorset's bedroom mere hours ago.

"I give everyone names," Charity responded breezily, entirely unconcerned. "Tiny suits you far better than Clementine does. And I don't find it overly warm. Do you, Vivi?"

The duchess cast a sidelong glance Clementine's way, clearly weighing her response with caution. "It is warm enough," she hedged.

"Perhaps Tiny is warm because she's been cavorting with a certain marquess."

"Charity, hush," Clementine warned. "Someone will overhear you."

"No one is around, save the three of us," Charity pointed out.

It was true that they were arriving at the lawn chess half an hour earlier than the prescribed time and that the rest of the guests were likely still preparing in their respective chambers. However, Clementine didn't want to take any chances. Particularly not where Dorset was concerned.

She couldn't abide the man. He was arrogant and smug, and he had a thoroughly wrongheaded dislike of her. That nettled—his scorn for her. *Loathe is rather a strong word*, he had said when she had accused him of loathing her. However, his protest had been markedly unconvincing, and even that had stung.

"Still, I don't want anyone to know," she told Charity. "If anyone were to find out…"

She shuddered, allowing her words to trail away.

"What were you doing in his chamber, again?" Vivi asked.

"I thought it was Charity's," she admitted, wincing as she recalled the instant her mistake had become known to her, along with the horror that had followed when she'd realized her discovery was imminent.

"Did you not read the name placards, dearest?" Charity asked.

"Clearly not," she muttered. "Pray, forget I ever told the two of you about my ignominious attempt at startling Charity and ending up in the wrong chamber."

She hadn't mentioned the rest of what had happened within those four walls.

"So, you hid behind the curtains," Charity said, "and Dorset immediately saw your feet peeping beneath them. What else happened?"

She fanned herself wildly. "Nothing. I apologized—not before Lady Edith and her mother wandered by below—and made a hasty retreat."

"Hmm." Charity regarded her with a narrow-eyed, searching look.

"What does that mean?" she asked, even though she knew she shouldn't.

That she should make every effort to divert their conversation to a safer subject. Because while she had shared her humiliation at her mistake with her friends, she hadn't said a word about all those devastating kisses she had shared with Dorset. Kisses that even now made her stomach feel strange and her body feel achy and needful at the mere thought of them.

"It means I don't believe you," Charity said with characteristic bluntness. "You're blushing, and it's plain to see that something has you quite overset."

"Was Dorset untoward?" Vivi asked, frowning. "I've always found him to be pleasant and respectful company despite his rakish reputation. I was hoping he could be depended upon to support the Lady's Suffrage Society, but if he did anything even the slightest bit offensive, tell me now and we'll send him back to the train station at once."

Clementine had no doubt that her loyal friend would indeed send the marquess away on her behalf. Oddly, the notion of his leaving the house party had her feeling bereft.

"He was the perfect gentleman," she hastened to reassure Vivi, even if that wasn't entirely the case.

He certainly hadn't kissed her like a perfect gentleman. He had kissed like a perfect sinner. A practiced seducer. A rake of the first order.

And she had liked it.

"You're certain?" Vivi persisted.

"No," she choked out, before belatedly realizing her friend wasn't privy to her thoughts. "That is, yes," she added, her voice an octave higher than usual.

"Something happened that you aren't telling us about," Charity said, her voice knowing as they turned onto the gravel path leading to the north lawns where the chess game was to be held. "You only sound that way when you're fibbing."

Ahead of them, a massive chessboard had been painted

carefully on the neatly kept grass. Standing at the edge of the tableau were two figures who were instantly recognizable. Clementine leapt at the chance for distraction.

"Oh, look," she said brightly, "it's Miss Madeline and Miss Lucy Chartrand."

The American sisters were fantastically wealthy heiresses who hailed from New York City. They had recently begun circulating in London Society, and it was rumored that their parents were intent upon them making advantageous matches with impoverished aristocrats. If rumors were to be believed, the Marquess of Dorset would make an excellent catch for either lady.

The notion made Clementine's stomach go sour.

She fanned herself furiously.

"They're early for our chess game," Vivi remarked, clearly distracted by her duties as hostess.

"I don't believe you, Tiny," Charity said quietly, like a dog with a bone. "He kissed you, didn't he?"

Good heavens, was it that obvious?

Her ears went hot. "Of course not."

"You can tell us the truth," her friend persisted. "We won't say a word to anyone else."

"The Chartrand sisters are coming toward us," Clementine hissed. "Cease interrogating me like a Scotland Yard detective, if you please."

Charity harumphed. "I can tell when you're lying, you know. Your voice gets higher than normal."

Clementine bit her lip.

"And you bite your lip," Charity added.

"Damn and blast," Clementine burst out. "He kissed me. There, are you satisfied?"

"I knew it," her friend crowed.

"What did you know?" asked Miss Madeline Chartrand

with her signature American boldness, leaping into the conversation without preamble.

Oh heavens, the sisters were upon them now.

"Nothing," Clementine and Charity said in unison.

The sisters shared a look.

"Let's discuss the Lady's Suffrage Society," Vivi suggested. "I've been hoping to chat with you ladies about joining us for our next meeting in London. The two of you would make an excellent addition to our ranks. The chess game won't start for another half hour. Shall we sit?"

She gestured toward a seating area that had been arranged near the chessboard. Vivi always thought of everything, and her house parties were unparalleled. In the past year, Clementine had grown quite close with the duchess as they bonded over their mutual cause.

"We would love to join your meeting," Miss Lucy Chartrand said.

"I wholeheartedly believe in the enfranchisement of women," Miss Madeline Chartrand added. "Lucy and I are members of a suffrage group at home in New York City."

"It would be lovely to join one here as well." Lucy beamed.

Vivi's plan of attracting new members to the Lady's Suffrage Society was unfolding as planned. If only Clementine's time at the house party were the same. She'd intended to mingle with friends, perhaps engage in some matchmaking if she found any couples amenable to it. Certainly *not* to kiss the Marquess of Dorset.

As if reading her mind, Charity raised a brow at Clementine, wordlessly warning her that she wouldn't be able to avoid further conversation about Dorset forever. Clementine schooled her expression into one of careful blankness, for she had no intention of discussing those heated kisses ever again.

Or thinking of them.

But as she and the ladies walked together to the chairs and tables, she couldn't seem to keep the memory of Dorset's mouth on hers from her mind, nor the way his tall, strong body had felt beneath her. Nor could she entirely banish the surge of longing rising within her, longing she hadn't felt in years.

Not since Walter.

And that, coupled with the burning memory of Dorset's mouth on hers, was what frightened Clementine most.

CHAPTER 4

Where was a convenient glass of Sauternes when he needed one?

Lady Clementine Hammond's kisses were haunting Ambrose as he found his way to the path that led to the massive maze—one of the crowning elements of the Sherborne Manor gardens, aside from the sunken fountain with its Venus and cavorting cupids. If he could not get lost in wine, then at least he could garner a respite from the maddening woman he couldn't seem to remove from his thoughts. Getting lost in a maze was preferable to continuing on with the game of life-sized chess currently unfolding on the north lawn.

Because *she* was there. Laughing, sweeping around the painted grass as if she were a queen descended amongst mere mortals, the sun catching in her dark hair beneath her ridiculously large picture hat and revealing hints of burnished gold. Looking somehow utterly sumptuous in a garish gown festooned with silk flowers and flounces.

He had nearly collided with her at one point, rendering his escape a necessity. Apparently, in addition to possessing a singular proficiency at kissing and making his cock hard, the irritating woman also had a complete lack of grace. He shouldn't have been surprised. She had, essentially, tackled him in his chamber.

Ambrose reached the head of the maze and disappeared within. He hoped there were benches somewhere, for he intended to settle his arse down and enjoy a peaceful cigar where he couldn't offend any feminine sensibilities. And forget all about Lady Clementine's body on his, her tempting curves molding to him in all the right places, her soft lips moving over his with greedy hunger, her tongue sliding sinuously into his mouth...

"Bloody hell," he cursed to himself.

He wasn't meant to be thinking of her. He was meant to be forgetting her. He didn't even *like* her. So why the devil did he want her so badly?

Crunch, crunch, crunch went his steps on the gravel path. He turned left, then right, then left again, thinking he would recall his path with ease, should he arrive at a dead end. The sky was bright blue overhead, speckled with fat white clouds. The sun was warm.

The farther he traveled from the gathering, the more his tensions eased. He made some more turns. *Right, right, left, right.* The fresh air of the country was always excellent. He might distract himself by riding, fishing, engaging in sport.

Finding the wine and drinking it all.

As he moved, the specter of the manor house loomed over him, tall, wide, imposing. He tried to gauge the direction he should take next and found himself blocked off by shrubbery.

Devil take it.

He turned back to the path. How had he arrived here? Right, left, right? Left, right, left?

"Damn," he muttered.

FOREVER HER MARQUESS

And that was when he heard it.

The screaming.

Apparently, a shred of him remained within that was gentlemanly and gallant. Because he started running in the direction of the ungodly sounds. And he didn't stop until he arrived at the source.

Lady Clementine Hammond stood in the midst of the path in a froth. Her hat was askew, and she was wailing while clutching handfuls of yellow silk. Aside from her dudgeon, nothing appeared to be wrong. He stopped just short of her. Had she followed him?

His eyes narrowed in suspicion.

"What is wrong?" he demanded curtly, watching as she shook her skirts and danced about.

"Bee!" she cried wildly.

Irritation surged. All this caterwauling because she had seen a damned bee? The woman was a menace.

"We are out of doors, madam," he informed her dryly as she continued her odd display. "Insects are to be expected."

Her blue eyes were wild as they met his, and she continued flouncing her skirts. "It's flown up my dress. What if it stings me?"

It would serve her right.

He bit his lip to keep from laughing at her antics. The horror on her countenance was, he could not lie, a small source of pleasure after the state of frustration her visit to his chamber had left him in.

"Help me," she implored.

"Double damn," he said under his breath.

There was no help for it. He was going to have to toss up Lady Clementine's skirts. The prospect wasn't an unpleasant one, he couldn't lie. Indeed, he'd been thinking of nothing but getting under her gown since she'd kissed the breath out of him.

Or I could allow her to get stung.

With great effort, Dorset silenced the evil voice within, summoning instead his pitiful sense of chivalry.

He started forward. "Calm yourself, Lady Clementine. The more you thrash, the greater the harm your bee shall believe himself to be in. The more likely he thinks you are to crush him, the more determined he shall be to defend himself."

"It's buzzing!" she cried, ignoring his warning as she whipped her skirts about with a violence that was guaranteed to get her stung. "Oh good heavens!"

He seized her hands with his, forcing her to still. Her horror was evident. Her breathing was harsh, as if she had run all the way to York Minster and back to Sherborne Manor.

"Hold still," he ordered her. "I'm going to raise your skirts, and hopefully the bee shall fly off, the both of you unscathed."

"No!" Her denial was swift. "You mustn't do that."

He ignored her. One of them had to be rational. That person was clearly not going to be the shrieking woman dressed like a garden that had vomited upon itself. He caught twin handfuls of silk and lifted.

But she would not remain immobile. The instant her hem lifted to reveal her pretty calves, lovingly encased in silk stockings, she twisted away from him. And then howled in pain.

"It stung me! The little devil stung me!"

Bloody hell. If it had been a honeybee beneath her skirts, the devil in question could have only stung her once. But if it was a wasp...

"Cease moving before it stings you again," he barked out, his patience for her growing smaller by the moment.

He lifted her skirts to her knees and shook out the voluminous layers.

"It smarts," she said with a rather pathetic whimper.

There were any number of jokes he could have made, but he did not think they would fall on appreciative ears, particularly since she would find herself the butt of them. He bit his tongue, keeping his attention upon her skirts, half expecting a swarm of angry bees to pour forth.

Instead, nothing happened.

The insect in question must have indeed been a honeybee. Satisfied after several rounds of shaking her skirts, he took note of a nearby stone bench and guided her toward it. With the initial terror of the bee removed, she was far more subdued. He had her settled on her rump and was on his knees before her on the gravel path, still playing the gentleman, albeit more reluctantly.

Up went her hems. "Show me where the little imp got you," he said.

~

CLEMENTINE NEVER SHOULD HAVE WANDERED into Vivi's blasted hedge labyrinth. She should have remained where she had been perfectly safe, playing at chess. But after her team's loss, her interest had waned, and she'd decided to take a quiet stroll in the maze. Now, her inner thigh throbbed, awash with a searing, burning pain. Through the miasma that had overtaken her mind, she became aware of the Marquess of Dorset's words.

"Show me where the little imp got you." He was persistently lifting her skirts once more.

Good heavens. She could not allow him to do so, regardless of the pain radiating from the cursed bee sting. Of all the days she had chosen to forgo her drawers, why, Lord in heaven, *why* had it had to be this one?

"That won't be necessary," she told him, trying to free her gown from his grasp. "I'll return to my chamber and see to the injury myself. Your intervention is no longer required."

"You've been stung," he said.

His eyes were a mysterious, inviting shade of green, she thought, and not for the first time.

Stop staring into his eyes, you ninny.

Where was her common sense when she needed it? How was it possible to experience such stinging agony and yet still take note of how handsome her reluctant savior was? To think about the way he had kissed her so urgently, until she had feared she might catch flame.

"I am aware that I was stung," she snapped, irritated with herself for being so affected by him and with the bee for landing her in such a predicament. "The pain radiating through me leaves no question of that."

His expression was one of distaste, as if he wished himself anywhere else, but he felt obligated by his gentlemanly sense of honor to aid her. Well, the feeling of dislike was decidedly mutual.

"If the stinger is indeed embedded in your flesh, it must be removed, Lady Clementine," he was saying, his tone almost patronizing.

"I was stung in a most indiscreet place," she hissed.

Also, I am not wearing drawers, you stubborn beast.

But she did not dare admit the last aloud. He had already managed to lift her skirts to her knees, where the crisp, white cotton of her undergarments should have shielded her from his gaze. Any higher, and he would have no doubt. It was scandalous, she knew. She never should have listened to Charity's advice. She wouldn't have done, had she not been so overset and overheated.

"Indiscreet," he repeated, his shoulders stiffening, jaw tensing.

"As I said." She tugged at her skirts again, still trying to wrestle them from his stubborn grasp. "There's no need for you to trouble yourself. When the pain lessens, I'll return to my chamber and see the injury tended to."

"The pain will not lessen if the stinger is lodged."

He was being logical. She knew the truth of his words. She had been stung as a girl, when she had been flitting barefoot through the lawns of Marchingham Hall. Stepped on a honeybee. Her governess had tended to the foot, because, of course, neither Mother nor Father had been in residence…

She shook her head, as if to clear the ghosts of the past. The marquess was once more fighting with her skirts. "I will remove the stinger in my chamber."

"And you intend to walk back to your chamber with the stinger in place?" he asked skeptically, nodding over his shoulder toward the looming architecture of Sherborne Manor house. It would indeed be a walk to her chamber, all whilst her thighs rubbed together in most uncomfortable fashion, the painful bee sting being mercilessly chafed with each step.

"Yes," she told him anyway. "You may leave me to my misery, Lord Dorset. I shall find my way back to my chamber as swiftly as possible on my own. Or mayhap you might be kind enough to locate the Duchess of Bradford for me and let her know of my plight. She may send a servant to aid me."

"Our hostess is undoubtedly busy with a great many other worries," Dorset said, his tone grim. "Cease protesting. The sooner this is done, the better for the both of us."

With that pronouncement, he flipped up her skirts suddenly and unexpectedly. She didn't have the chance to shield herself.

Warm summer's air kissed her naked thighs. And her naked...*elsewhere*.

"My lord!" she exclaimed, pressing her thighs together and then crying out in pain as the bee sting reminded her of its presence.

"Lord Dorset!"

"Clementine?"

"Tiny?"

The interrupting voices made her heart plummet. A group of fellow guests barreled around the corner of the maze. Vivi was at the vanguard, with her husband not far behind. Charity, Lady Edith Smythe, and the Chartrand sisters were at their heels, and good heavens, was that the odious Lady Featherstone at the rear? Everything inside her shriveled at the unwanted audience.

Meanwhile, there Clementine sat, her skirts rucked about her waist, the Marquess of Dorset on his knees before her. Her mortification was complete. And the last words he had said, lest anyone had overheard? *The sooner this is done, the better for the both of us.*

To say nothing of her lack of drawers.

She fumbled with her silk and petticoats, struggling to draw them into place. Dorset reacted with much more haste than her addled mind was currently able to manage. He flipped her gown down all the way, until no part of her was on display, and then rose, turning to face their sudden company.

Why had she not worn drawers? If any of them had seen her most intimate flesh—Lord Dorset included—Clementine was sure she would die a swift and humiliated death.

It is exceedingly hot out, Charity had told her with the effortless lack of concern only Lady Charity Manners possessed. *I never wear drawers in the summer. Layers are despicable and stifling. Summer is a time of freedom from the tyranny of strict dressing rules, Tiny.* And Clementine had been persuaded. But now...

Well.

Clearly, her dear finishing school chum Charity had never been caught with a bee up her skirts or her gown raised and a man on his knees before her during those times of summer freedom.

"Lady Clementine has been stung by a bee," Dorset announced to the shocked house party guests gaping at them. "I was coming to her aid, and I...forgot myself. Especially after she had agreed, in the seconds before the bee sting, to become my wife."

Clementine had been following the marquess's speech, pleased by his deflection. Up until that very last bit.

To become my wife.

Wife?

What the devil?

The urge to kick him in his bottom—which she took that moment to observe was finely formed, even beneath the tails of his tweed coat—was tempting, indeed.

She cleared her throat. "My lord."

He ignored her. "Forgive me, Your Graces, but the love Lady Clementine and I share is too strong. Indeed, I cannot help but to think your house party has facilitated the blossoming of this wondrous love between us. I cannot express my gratitude enough. Until my arrival here, I was convinced I would never love again. You have proven me wrong."

No, no, no.

That was a lie.

A terrible, smoothly spoken, despicable lie.

"I was never capable of fathoming such devoted, soul-buoying love," the scoundrel continued.

What was this? Had he *intended* to ruin her? Was he in need of the dowry her father increased with every Season she failed to wed? There was no other explanation for his reaction.

She aimed a kick to the back of Dorset's knee.

And missed. Blast her legs. Too short. Always, forever too short. And in pain. She bit back a muffled cry of agony.

"In love," Vivi proclaimed, peering around the marquess and giving Clementine a searching look. "Truly?"

"How dreadful for such a happy occasion to be interrupted by a bee sting," Lady Edith said kindly before Clementine could answer, her eyes wide behind her spectacles.

Lady Featherstone was indeed at the rear of the little group, and she made her presence known by issuing a sniff of disdain. "In my day, it was quite forbidden for a young gentleman courting a lady to be alone with her."

"Dorset isn't courting me," Clementine began explaining, fully intending to disabuse everyone of the marquess's ludicrous claim.

"My future marchioness means to say that our courting is now at an end, given our engagement," the marquess interjected smoothly. "But for now, I do think it in the best interest of Lady Clementine that she make haste to her chamber, all the better for her to seek proper treatment of her sting. She suffered the injury on her limb, you see, and is now unable to walk."

My future marchioness.

Clementine was seriously considering boxing his ears for uttering such outrageous falsehoods. Vivi and Charity were close, dear friends, and she trusted the Duke of Bradford to keep a secret, but the American heiresses were still relatively new acquaintances, as was Lady Edith. And Clementine shuddered to think of the gossip Lady Featherstone would spread.

"I'll carry my betrothed to her chamber," Dorset announced confidently.

"I can walk there on my own," she protested, thinking of how far they were from her chamber. How difficult it would prove for even a man as broad-shouldered and well-formed as the marquess to haul her that lengthy distance.

"Nonsense, my darling beloved," Dorset said through gritted teeth as he turned toward Clementine, giving her a forced smile. "I shall see you safely returned to your chamber. Duchess, as our hostess, perhaps you might choose a chaperone to accompany us in the interest of propriety?"

"That won't be necessary," Clementine protested quietly, painfully aware of their audience.

It was a bit late to consider propriety, she thought grimly. There had been the matter of their kissing in his bedroom, and now he had been caught beneath her skirts, and with the Marchioness of Featherstone as witness to it all.

"Clementine?" Vivi prodded, her brow furrowed. "Are you in very much pain, my dear? It is very gallant of Lord Dorset to offer to carry you back, unless you would prefer the assistance of a footman?"

She would prefer for the ground to open up with a convenient hole in which she could hide herself. Her thigh still throbbing, along with her pride, Clementine had no recourse, save allowing the Marquess of Dorset to scoop her into his arms. He had just announced to everyone that they were in love and that he had proposed. If she requested a footman to carry her, tongues would wag.

"Very gallant, indeed," she echoed faintly. "Dorset will do."

He bent and took her into his arms with surprising ease. Clementine suddenly found herself aloft, clutching at his broad shoulders for purchase. Alarmingly near to his handsome face and his sensual lips.

Sensual lips? What was she thinking?

She ought to be ashamed of herself.

"Would anyone like to accompany Lord Dorset and Lady Clementine to her chamber?" Vivi asked.

"I'll go with them," Lady Edith offered hastily.

And her heart sank, for surely Lady Edith only wanted gossip to carry back to her dragon of a mother.

Clementine was doomed.

CHAPTER 5

*L*ady Clementine was a petite woman, and Dorset generally considered himself a sporting fellow, one who took pride in his athleticism. But by the time he reached the front hall of Sherborne Manor, Lady Edith trailing behind chattering about antiquities, Lady Clementine and her monstrosity of a dress in his arms, he was decidedly out of breath. So out of breath that he needed to pause and settle his new betrothed upon her feet.

"I can travel the rest of the way on my own," she huffed, the first words she had issued to him during their travels from the maze.

She appeared nettled. Excellent. He hoped she was. He did not like the troublesome baggage. She had caused all manner of difficulty for him, both past and present. To say nothing of the countless others whose lives she had affected with her meddling. She ought to have been stung by a hundred bees rather than just the one.

When he could catch his breath, he would give her his opinion on the matter.

"...the Roman ruins."

Blast. He turned to find Lady Edith standing at their side with an expectant expression. Behind her spectacles, her blue eyes glittered with excitement, and he could not deny the red-haired woman was lovely. However, he did not give a damn about history. Which explained why he had allowed most of the lady's soliloquy to be drowned out by his own thoughts.

And mayhap the ragged nature of his inhalations.

"Yes," he managed to mutter in her direction. "The ruins. Fascinating."

His bloody forehead was sweating.

"There are Roman ruins here?" Lady Clementine asked, sounding intrigued.

"Yes, along with a castle as well, which was abandoned several centuries ago, according to Her Grace," Lady Edith confirmed with a shy smile. "I would dearly love to investigate both, if *Maman* will permit it."

"If your mother doesn't permit it, might you not simply slip away on your own when she's having a nap?" Lady Clementine suggested.

Lady Edith's smile deepened, revealing dimples. "I daresay you've read my thoughts, Lady Clementine."

It occurred to Dorset that he was being ignored, and he wasn't certain he liked it. Particularly not from the woman he had just pretended to betroth himself to all for the sake of saving her from scandal. To say nothing of having transported her from the garden to this very spot in the great hall.

"Do you think it wise to run wild about Sherborne Manor?" he asked Lady Edith, but he was looking at Lady Clementine. "Doing so certainly seems potentially ruinous."

Her nostrils flared, and she caught her lush lower lip between her teeth. He wondered if she was thinking about their interlude in his chamber earlier. God knew he'd thought of precious little since, much to his chagrin.

Lady Edith issued a long-suffering sigh. "Only if one is caught, I suppose."

Caught. As Ambrose and Clementine had been. Bloody hell, he would have to think of a way to work the both of them out of this terrible mire. He couldn't marry her. Wouldn't dream of doing so. Kissing a woman was one matter. Being bound to her for life was entirely another.

"Oh dear," Lady Edith hastened to say, pressing a hand over her heart, her cheeks going red. "I am forever saying the wrong thing. *Maman* despairs of me, and I can't blame her. Forgive me, Lord Dorset, Lady Clementine. I didn't mean to suggest your betrothal was caused by the scene just now in the labyrinth."

"We aren't betrothed," Lady Clementine blurted, shooting Ambrose a pointed glare that, had it been a blade, would have left him bleeding on the marble floor.

"You aren't?" Lady Edith's brow furrowed.

"We are," he informed their unwanted chaperone.

At the same moment, Lady Clementine announced, "We most certainly are *not.*"

"Oh." Lady Edith blinked, the effect looking almost owlish behind her spectacles. "I own, I did wonder. You had seemed quite taken with Mr. Macfie."

Macfie? Surely not the Scot who was a business partner of Elijah Decker's. For a reason Dorset could not define, the knowledge irked him.

"Mr. Macfie was regaling me with a delightful tale of his youth that had me laughing so hard my sides ached," said Lady Clementine, apparently confirming Lady Edith's observation.

By God.

Had she kissed Mr. Macfie the way she had kissed him? Had she ventured into Mr. Macfie's bloody room? The very thought of it had jealousy arcing through him, bright and hot as electricity.

"Mr. Macfie did not carry you in his arms for a whole hectare because you had been stung by a bee," he reminded Lady Clementine. "To say nothing of this entire affair having been caused by your own foolishness. First in wearing that ridiculous garb and then in strutting about a garden without the proper undergarments."

Lady Edith gave a quiet gasp.

Ah, hell. He hadn't meant to say the last aloud. Hadn't intended to draw attention to the fact that beneath her wretched gown had lain a paradise of silk stockings, frothy garters, and naught else. The memory of her bare thighs should not make his cock twitch to life in his trousers at this very moment. Particularly not whilst he was standing in the Sherborne Manor great hall with an audience.

But it did.

Truly, he despised her. But he was also a man. And it turned out that a certain portion of his anatomy did not mind whom the glimpse of forbidden flesh he had spied earlier belonged to.

Down, old chap. We have a more-than-trustworthy hand to aid our cause.

"How dare you speak of my undergarments before Lady Edith?" Lady Clementine pursed her lips, her shoulders going back with defiance. "Furthermore, it was scarcely any distance from the gardens to here, and I never asked you to carry me."

"I have caught my breath," he announced with grim intent. "Let us carry on."

The sooner he deposited Lady Clementine at the door to her chamber, where she could become someone else's problem, the better. He did not know why he had volunteered

FOREVER HER MARQUESS

himself for this painful act of gallantry. But now that he had, he meant to see it through.

"I told you that I'll walk," the lady in question said, her countenance mulish. "Lady Edith will accompany me. Will you not, my dear?"

Lady Edith's brows inched up her forehead, above the gold rims of her spectacles. "Of course I will, but if you are in pain, perhaps you should accept Lord Dorset's offer of aid."

"I shall survive," Lady Clementine declared. "Anything to hasten Lord Dorset's return to the other houseguests, so that he may explain he was only joking when he announced we would be married."

Perversely, the more agitated she became by his nonsensical ramblings earlier, the more pleased he found himself. Initially, he had offered the explanation in the interest of blunting scandal and gossip, with the idea they could easily extricate themselves from their "betrothal" before the house party's end. But he could not deny he found something remarkably delicious about watching Lady Clementine squirm, caught in one of her own snares for the first time.

"I will do nothing of the sort," he told her, then promptly swept her back into his arms before she could offer further protestation.

"Put me down, you barbarian!"

He ignored Lady Clementine's cry, directing his attention to their unlikely chaperone instead. "Lead the way, Lady Edith."

"Oh." She pushed her spectacles up the bridge of her freckled nose. "I…of course. Right this way, my lord."

∽

STILL MISERABLE FROM the bee sting she had suffered on her inner thigh in the maze, Clementine watched from the periphery of the Sherborne Manor conservatory as her fellow guests whirled about the flora and fauna.

Vivi had decreed each evening of the fortnight-long house party be spent in revelry. Tonight's offering, a country dance, was only serving to heighten Clementine's gloom. Because watching Dorset twirl about the chamber with Madeline Chartrand—his present partner—was decidedly irksome.

Also, silly.

Despite his earlier pronouncement to the members of the house party who had happened upon them in the garden, they were most certainly not betrothed. And if rumors were to be believed, Dorset needed the funds an American heiress could bring him with her dowry. They made a perfect couple, both of them dark-haired, Miss Chartrand elegant as she sailed about the conservatory in perfect time with the marquess.

Perhaps Clementine ought to try her matchmaking hand with Dorset and Miss Chartrand.

But first, she had to make it known that she was not, under any circumstances, marrying the marquess. And how to do so without landing herself in more scandal? In attempting to avoid making tongues wag, Dorset had certainly created a dreadful conundrum for which she had no solution.

Clementine bit her lip to suppress a derisive snort as she watched everyone else enjoying themselves. Even Charity was dancing, and with Viscount Wilton, who was a dreadfully proper bore. Miss Chartrand was laughing at something Dorset said. Why had Clementine never noticed how beautiful the American heiress was before now?

She frowned as an unwanted pang of what felt rather alarmingly like jealousy winged through her. It was not that she had any claims upon Dorset. Nor that she wanted to marry him. *Certainly not.* Handsome, silver-tongued rakes were deplorable creatures. And a handsome, silver-tongued rake who appeared *amused* when she had been stung by a bee? One who had gone on to pretend they were engaged? She wouldn't even think about how proficient a kisser he was, nor the clever way he had made her insides melt with his skillful lips, how tempting his strong, muscled frame had been under hers.

For now, Dorset's deceptions were all she could think upon, a likely ploy to obtain her dowry. Or something more nefarious.

The devil himself could be no worse.

And yet…

"Hmm," she grumbled to herself, feeling quite displeased —and irrationally so—as Miss Chartrand and Dorset continued on.

"Your betrothed and Miss Chartrand dance together quite gracefully."

The voice, so near, gave Clementine a jolt. She turned to find Lady Edith at her side, gaze far too knowing behind her spectacles.

She was surprised that the dowager marchioness was not hovering at Lady Edith's elbow, prepared to breathe fire at any unfortunate gentleman who dared to have the effrontery to ask Lady Edith for a dance. Now that she thought upon it, Clementine wouldn't be averse to playing matchmaker for the shy wallflower.

Clementine worried her lip, formulating a careful answer, for she wasn't entirely certain she dared trust Lady Edith, despite her seemingly kind nature. "As I told you earlier, Lord Dorset isn't my betrothed. I hardly wish to bind myself forever to such a rogue."

"A rogue you cannot seem to wrest your eyes from," Lady Edith observed quietly.

Blast.

She tore her gaze, which had once more strayed to Dorset and the elder Miss Chartrand, back to the lady at her side. Vivi trusted Lady Edith, and Clementine trusted Vivi's judgment implicitly. She would have confided in her dear friend herself, but Vivi had recently been reunited with the duke, who had been abroad for the last year. The two of them had reconciled in the past few weeks and had become virtually inseparable. Between the distraction of her husband and her hostess duties for the house party, Vivi had been too busy for Clementine to arrange a tête-à-tête.

And she was in desperate need of a confidante.

"He was lying in the labyrinth, you know," she confided. "Likely trying to cause trouble for me."

"The marquess?" Lady Edith frowned thoughtfully. "He appeared to be trying to aid you."

What a good-hearted, naïve dear Lady Edith was.

Clementine made a dismissive wave of her fingertips. "If he truly wished to aid me, he would never have spouted that nonsense about the two of us becoming engaged."

"It seemed he did so to preserve your reputation."

What was this? Lady Edith continued to see the best in the Marquess of Dorset?

Oh no. *Heavens* no.

"He is a rakehell of the worst order," she informed Lady Edith. "His reputation precedes him."

And his kisses certainly spoke for themselves.

Delicious.

She struck the unwanted thought from her mind at once.

"He did appear quite concerned with your welfare for a callous rake," Lady Edith countered.

She pinned the other woman with a narrow-eyed glare. "Trust me, my lady. No one can recognize a rake more easily than I, having been the victim of one myself."

The moment she made the revelation, she cursed herself inwardly for mentioning one of the most painful times in her life. Four years had passed, but her bitterness over Walter's cruel treatment of her remained. She had believed herself in love. How wrong she'd been. Rakes were selfish, vile hedonists concerned far more with their own pleasure than the feelings of the women with whom they toyed. Like a big cat pawing at an innocent mouse, Walter had inflicted much damage upon her. His handsome charm had lured her in, and she'd been too foolish to realize the snake lurking beneath his gentlemanly façade.

Lady Edith frowned. "Forgive me. It wasn't my intention to cause you distress. The marquess seemed determined to see to your comfort. That is all I meant to say."

Yes, Dorset *had* carried her all the way to her chamber, depositing her at the threshold before taking his leave so that her lady's maid could aid her in assuaging the pain of the sting. But she was not inclined to believe it had been because he had truly cared about her well-being. Likely, it was something far more selfish at work, like any true rake.

"It was an attempt at preserving his own honor," she said. "Nothing more. I consider myself fortunate indeed that we are not truly betrothed."

"And yet, you are glowering at his lordship as he dances a quadrille with another lady," Lady Edith pointed out with a shrewdness that belied her customarily timid demeanor.

Apparently, when she was beyond the reach of her dragon mama, Lady Edith was rather outspoken. Hmm. Perhaps there was hope for her yet and she would join the Lady's Suffrage Society as Vivi hoped.

"I would never glower at Miss Chartrand," Clementine lied brightly. For in truth, she might, should the circumstances warrant a stern glower. "I assure you, I'm reserving all my glares for the marquess."

"I'm reasonably sure Madeline hasn't eyes for Dorset," Lady Edith said. "You needn't worry on that score."

"And how can you be so certain?" She gave the lady at her side a pointed look.

What did Lady Edith know that she did not? Had the elder Miss Chartrand confided in her?

Lady Edith flushed, her lips firming. "I cannot be, of course."

A lie if Clementine had ever heard one.

Her brows snapped together, her inner matchmaker awakening as relief she refused to acknowledge washed over her. "Madeline Chartrand has set her cap at someone, then? Someone she has mentioned to you? Are the two of you friends?"

A most interesting development, indeed. Clementine would have thought the American heiresses moved in far too fast a set for Lady Featherstone's liking. But it seemed that Lady Edith possessed a certain knowledge. A confidence, even. And that Miss Madeline Chartrand was not setting her cap at Dorset. Not that Clementine cared if any of the unattached ladies present were casting their matrimonial wiles in the marquess's direction, Miss Chartrand included. For she did not. Not a whit.

Very well.

Maybe a tiny speck.

No! She banished the thought. If only she could banish *him*. But there he remained, dark-haired and tall, dancing about with Madeline Chartrand, wielding his sensual grin upon her. He was handsome, the Marquess of Dorset. Insufferably, irritatingly so.

"I do know that her mother is quite set upon her ensnaring herself a duke and not a lowly marquess," Lady Edith said, sighing with a touch of bitterness. "As all matchmaking mamas do."

It would seem Miss Chartrand had confided in Lady Edith. At least in a small measure.

"And is Lady Featherstone seeking a duke for you as well, then?" Clementine asked, curious. "Should you not be dancing with the rest of the guests if finding a match is your aim?"

Lady Edith shrugged. "It may be my mother's aim, but it most certainly isn't mine. I came here to see the Roman ruins and learn more about the Lady's Suffrage Society. Pray, don't tell *Maman* that, however. She is most pleased at the prospect of marrying me off forthwith."

The plot grew more intriguing by the moment. Perhaps Lady Edith had a spine after all. Good for her.

Clementine fanned herself and forced her gaze to keep from straying to the Marquess of Dorset. "Will you join our cause? Vivi is determined to bring as many members into the fold as possible. That is why Lady Josephine Decker, the Countess of Sinclair, and the Duchess of Bainbridge are in attendance, you know. This is an informal meeting, I suppose. Only, with dancing and life-size lawn chess."

"One can never discount the importance of life-size lawn chess," Lady Edith drawled.

"Or dancing."

They grinned at each other, and Clementine decided she liked Lady Edith very much. There was far more to her than met the eye. But then, Vivi was an excellent judge of character.

The quadrille ended, and to her dismay, Clementine discovered the Marquess of Dorset was approaching their quiet corner of the conservatory. His verdant gaze connected with hers.

"It appears as if your betrothed is in need of an audience," Lady Edith said, *sotto voce*.

"We are *not* betrothed," she grumbled.

But she could not seem to tear her stare from Dorset as he sauntered to them. How was it that the manner in which the man *walked* could transfix her? His legs were long, his shoulders wide. *He has a reputation as a dreadful rake,* she reminded herself. And after Walter, she had vowed she would never again fall beneath the spell of a handsome, charming roué.

Despite her inner warnings, the memory of Dorset's scent, rich and musky, hit her. She had been tempted to bury her face in his throat to inhale deeply on more than one occasion during their impromptu trip from the maze. She had also found herself ridiculously fascinated by the shadow of whiskers on the slashing angle of his jaw.

He reached them and bowed. "Lady Clementine, Lady Edith. We meet again."

She dipped into an abbreviated curtsy thanks to her smarting thigh, Lady Edith following suit. "Good evening, Lord Dorset."

"I wonder if I might borrow my betrothed for a turn around the room." Dorset addressed Lady Edith, as if she were Clementine's keeper.

In truth, her intended chaperone for the house party, her mother, was in Derbyshire for Clementine's elder sister's lying in. Clementine had proceeded on to Sherborne Manor in her absence, arriving well before the house party had begun. The arrangement had suited her fine, and she'd even been afforded the chance to play matchmaker for Vivi and her husband. It was plain to see they were madly in love, and Clementine had been happy to facilitate their reconciliation.

"Of course you may borrow her," Lady Edith said with a cheeky wink for Clementine.

So much for thinking she liked Lady Edith. Before Clementine could offer argument, the bespectacled lady quickly took her leave. Which meant Clementine stood alone with Dorset, whose delicious, manly scent was every bit as delightful to her senses this evening as it had previously been. *Curse him.* Why was he standing so near?

"I am not your betrothed," Clementine grumbled at Dorset when Lady Edith was gone.

"Yes, you are," he argued, his tone smooth, his countenance imperturbable.

She wanted to irritate him. To ruffle his feathers. She wanted to be the bee who gave him a sting.

"Do you have a need for my dowry?" she asked bluntly.

The corners of his finely sculpted lips twitched as if he were attempting to suppress a grin. "Your lack of tact rivals your lack of drawers, I see."

His words made her cheeks go hot. "Of all the despicable things you might have said, that is by far the worst you could have chosen."

"Despicable?" This time, he did grin. "I am not the one gadding about the gardens without proper undergarments."

The utter bounder.

She cast a wary glance around them to make certain no one was near enough to overhear, but all their fellow guests were engaged in either dancing or socializing. "You are a scoundrel to mention it."

"You seem in a dreadful mood this evening, Lady Clementine." His gaze roamed over her face, taking her in. "Whatever is the matter? Could it be that you dislike finding yourself ensnared in the same trap in which you caught so many others?"

Ah. She began to understand him. This betrothal nonsense was not about his need for her dowry at all. Rather, it was a petty means of gaining his revenge. She was familiar with his former betrothed, Lady Anna Harcastle, who had married the Marquess of Huntly.

"The Marchioness of Huntly is desperately in love with the marquess," she told him.

His lips compressed, the hint of mirth vanishing. "According to you. Who do you think you are, playing with the lives of so many others? It is about time your life was toyed with a bit, rather in the fashion of a cat batting at a mouse."

"Am I to infer I am the mouse and you are the cat? Is this betrothal nonsense nothing but a game to you?"

"A game with a twofold purpose, my lady." He drew his hand along the jaw she had so admired when in his arms. "I must admit that I am enjoying your suffering. But also, whilst I have no intention of actually making you my marchioness, feigning a betrothal for the duration of the house party will save the both of us from scandal. As I'm in search of a suitable bride, I can't afford to go about ruining ladies, regardless of how dubious their honor may be."

She frowned at him, trying to ignore what he had said about enjoying her suffering and his casual questioning of her reputation. "You mean to break the engagement before the house party's end?"

"Yes. It is a simple enough plan, really. We wait long enough that everyone's collective memory has faded, and then we shall declare we no longer suit."

He was perfectly calm, as if certain she would agree to his scheme.

"No," she said.

"No?" His dark brows arched.

"I imagine that is not a word you are accustomed to hearing, Lord Dorset—"

"You are correct," he interjected. "It is not."

She glared at him as she continued. "*However*, I have no wish to participate in your plan. I'll not pretend to be your betrothed. Nor will I be your source of vindictive amusement."

"I am afraid you have no choice in the matter," the wicked marquess countered, grinning. "I've made certain every member of the house party is aware of our happy news."

Had she thought him a bounder earlier? That was far too generous. With a sinking sensation in her gut, she dragged her gaze back to the Marquess of Dorset, who was still grinning.

She had been wrong.

It was more than clear to her now that the Marquess of Dorset was the devil himself.

CHAPTER 6

In the welcoming confines of the Sherborne Manor library the next day, Clementine sighed with appreciation as she walked along the shelf-lined walls in search of something suitable to read. Vivi had settled upon a walk following breakfast for the morning's entertainment, and Clementine had seized upon her still-healing bee sting as the perfect excuse to remain behind.

And avoid Dorset as well.

She huffed with irritation as she thought of the manner in which he had made certain their sham betrothal would be announced, as if it were a happy occasion to be celebrated. How she would have liked to have stomped on his overly large foot. Yes, she had noticed the size of his shoes. Everything about the marquess was large. His hands, his height, his feet. Well, not his nose.

His nose was exceedingly fine, straight, and perfectly proportioned. Not that she had noticed.

"Drat the man," she muttered to herself.

He was a source of irritation even when he was no longer beneath the same roof, having gone off on the walk. As she passed the nearly floor-to-ceiling mullioned windows that looked out over the park, dark clouds threatening the horizon appeared an ominous portent of how the walk would end. If there was any justice in the world, Lord Dorset would find himself in the midst of a downpour. Soaked to the skin.

But curse him. Even that fantasy ended with thoughts of what he would look like with his crisp, white shirt sodden and clinging to his chest.

She passed a group of shelves where Roman artifacts—presumably from the Sherborne Manor ruins—were on display, and then moved to the final wall of books. There were no volumes catching her eye at the moment, despite the fact that Vivi possessed excellent taste in literature. Spying a ladder that led to the higher shelves, she decided to explore the books above.

But by the time she climbed to the rung that was third from the top, she realized the ladder was not properly planted on the rug as she reached for a spine and the ladder pitched beneath her movement. She clung wildly to the shelves, her heart leaping into her throat.

Dear sweet heavens. Her position was tenuous at best. One wrong move, and she would topple several feet to the floor below. A bee sting would be the least of her worries.

Stay calm. Stay still. Shift to the left.

She did, and the ladder tilted precariously.

With a cry, she scrambled for purchase. Her frantic fingers found leather tomes and shelf edges. Books dropped to the floor. Oh good Lord, now she was destroying her friend's books. Vivi had only just recently filled this library with books to her liking.

The carpets loomed far, far below. Clementine felt suddenly dizzy. She grasped at more books. These, too, fell. They rained to the floor in an eerie imitation of the impending precipitation she was sure would fall upon the house party guests who were out on their walk.

"Does your appetite for ruin know no end?"

The deep, familiar voice had her gasping and jerking toward its source. The Marquess of Dorset was strolling across the library toward her. Oh, what was the devil doing here? Why was he not on the walk with the rest of the guests?

She meant to issue a blistering response. But in the next moment, the ladder pitched, listing to the right, much like a ship in a storm-swept sea. As she scrambled to grab hold of something, she was certain she could right herself. But this time, her fingertips slid over smooth surfaces.

And she was falling.

Fear rose. A scream tore from her throat. The ceiling swam before her as she catapulted backward, heart pounding, her terrible landing undeniable until…

She landed in a familiar pair of arms.

The Marquess of Dorset made a grunting sound as he clutched her to him, sparing her from a terrible landing upon the floor. Saving her from injury. Cradling her against his broad, strong chest.

His warmth bit into her. She grasped his shoulders, acting instinctively.

"I have you," he said.

And for a moment, those words were the most reassuring and comforting she had ever heard. Until she realized who had spoken them.

Dorset.

A rake. A scoundrel. The man who resented her for having arranged the marriage between the Marquess of Huntly and the former Lady Anna Harcastle. The man who had insisted upon carrying on with a feigned betrothal.

The man who had commented upon her lack of drawers.

Untrustworthy.

Handsome.

Why was he so handsome?

She pulled her hands from his shoulders as if he had burned her, for he may as well have done. "Thank you for your gallantry, but I can stand upon my own two feet now."

"That is hardly the thanks I deserve for saving you from breaking your lovely neck, my darling betrothed."

Oh, he was truly terrible. A complex blend of beautiful and despicable. A handsome rake who did not shy away from gallantry, and yet one who also was using her in cruelest fashion. He wanted his revenge upon her. And she merely wanted to be left alone.

She wanted to visit with her dear friends, take in the country air, and then resume her life. She wanted to be a matchmaker, someone who facilitated happiness for others when she knew it was impossible to achieve herself. That was how she found contentment, setting others upon the path to marriage. The path fate and Walter's stinging betrayal had so cruelly denied her.

She said the first thing that came to her mind.

"I would not have broken my neck."

"So certain. What if I had not been here to catch you?" he asked.

Indeed. What if he had not been there to save her from landing upon the unforgiving floor? What if she had been injured, or worse?

From this perspective—held suspended in the Marquess of Dorset's arms for the second time—she could admit that she had been reckless with the ladder. She should have taken more time to make certain it was planted firmly on the floor. Instead, she had ignored her every instinct and gone plummeting to earth.

To Dorset.

"Why are you here?" she demanded. "The rest of the company has gone on a walk. I presumed you had joined them."

"And leave my beloved betrothed behind?" He sent her a rogue's unrepentant grin. "I could never."

Her eyes narrowed. "Put me down, you scoundrel, and cease referring to me as your betrothed."

"A scoundrel now, am I? Your gratitude is markedly short-lived, madam."

"As is your gallantry," she reminded pointedly, thinking of the bold manner in which he had referred to her lack of drawers.

Her cheeks stung anew at the memory.

"You are flushing quite prettily, Lady Clementine. Which makes me suspect you are thinking of what I saw beneath your elegant skirts."

Good God. Her face went hotter still. She had hoped he had seen nothing. And curse Charity for this disaster…

"How dare you make mention of something so indelicate?" She moved, attempting to free herself from his hold. "Put me down, if you please."

"I must admit, I grow rather fond of having you in my arms." His gaze dipped to her lips so fleetingly she may have imagined it.

Except for the tingling that told her his brilliant stare had indeed been upon her mouth.

This would not do.

She planted her palms on his chest and pushed. "I am decidedly *not* fond of being here. I have two perfectly functional limbs to aid me."

"And yet you declined to accompany the rest of the guests on today's walk." Once more, his tone was smooth. His expression bland.

He set her on her feet again and relief swept over her. She was freed of his heat, his strength, his scent.

"Thank you." She stepped away from him, needing the distance, and shook out her skirts, trying to calm her jagged nerves. "Of course I declined."

"Why?"

Had not Mama always told her honesty was preferable unless a polite lie would suffice?

"Because I wished to avoid you," she answered simply. No need to offer the Marquess of Dorset a polite lie.

If she could draw blood, she would.

He quirked a brow. "I thought you may have been suffering from the bee sting."

"Merely suffering from the desire to avoid your presence." She swept past him, determined to put as much of the Axminster between them as possible.

"I am wounded, darling betrothed."

Despite his words, she heard laughter in his voice. She cast a glance over her shoulder, which proved a mistake. He was following her, an amused grin on his ridiculous mouth. Truly, why had God bestowed such a sensual pair of lips upon yet another conscienceless rakehell?

"I am not your betrothed," she told him yet again. "Nor am I your darling. This argument grows wearisome."

"Then do not argue, Lady Clementine." He stalked nearer, invading her territory, until her back was pressed to a wall of books and he was near enough to touch. His hands landed on the spines on either side of her head, caging her in. "The answer is simple. No need to complicate things. I saved your reputation when I had neither desire nor obligation to do so. You owe me, and if the price I demand is watching you squirm in a trap of your own making, you shall have to pay it."

Drat the man. He was insistent upon playing out this

nonsensical plan of his. Every inhalation brought his decadent scent, tempting and teasing. She would not look at his lips. Would not think about how handsome he was...

A sudden idea came to her, forged of desperation. What would Dorset do if she decided to capitulate? If she pretended to be in favor of this noxious feigned betrothal of his?

Oh yes. Why had she not thought of this sooner? It was all she could do to suppress her smile. The marquess may have won the hand, but she would emerge the victor from this game they played.

～

"Mayhap you are right."

Ambrose blinked, sure he had misheard Lady Clementine. Those four words—a concession if he was correct, issued to him? Bloody impossible.

"I beg your pardon?"

She rolled her lips inward, pressing them together. His gaze was pinned upon that mouth. *Damn.* Why should such a vicious harpy have been blessed with lips even Venus would have had cause to covet? And why the devil should he find himself once more contemplating those same lips, wondering what they would feel like beneath his?

Pliant? Seductive as silk? Warm or cool? Would she kiss him in return, or would she hold still?

So many questions, all of them wrong. None of them should be infecting his mind. But try as he might, he could not seem to tamp down the rising tides of his lust for this woman.

"As you said, there is no need to complicate things," she said in a pleasant tone, her voice light, sweet. "You saved my reputation in the gardens. I do owe you, and if the price you demand is a betrothal, then I shall have to pay it until the house party is at an end."

His eyes narrowed. What was this? Lady Clementine Hammond agreeing with him, no longer prickly? Her lovely countenance was deceptively beatific. She was as glorious as a goddess, and yet he knew she was as duplicitous as a fallen angel.

"You have finally decided to see the sense in my proposal?" he asked hesitantly.

"Of course." She flashed him a bright smile that should not have hit him in the chest. Should not have made him go hard.

And yet it did.

No denying the effect this loathsome lady had upon him.

He hoped to hell his country tweed trousers were concealing his cockstand. He cleared his throat, then ran his hand along his jaw. Cleanly shaven that morning and already studded with whiskers. A reminder he was harsh. Not smooth, not soft.

Lady Clementine Hammond would do well to remember the same. How to remind her? He was so surprised by her sudden capitulation that he didn't know what the devil to say next.

"Then you agree to a betrothal for the duration of the house party?" he forced himself to ask at last.

"Yes. I concede to the wisdom of your plan. But I should call you something other than your title, if we are to make the others believe we are truly engaged. Do you not think? A pet name or diminutive, if you please."

Was that what she thought engaged couples did? They made stupid bloody names for each other? He suppressed a shudder. Preserve him from the nonsense of unmarried ladies everywhere.

"You should call me Dorset," he told her calmly. "That is what everyone calls me. *Because it is my name.*"

He spoke slowly, enunciating with care. Perhaps Lady Clementine was not the most intelligent specimen of the fairer sex. Mayhap she was a trifle touched. It would hardly be surprising. Why else would she take such great delight in fomenting the misery of others?

"Of course everyone calls you Dorset." She wiggled her fingers in a dainty, dismissive fashion. "But I am to be your *betrothed*. I should be on far-more-familiar terms with you than everyone else."

Was the woman mad, or was she a featherbrain? Or was this some sort of trick? He could not be certain. All he did know was that she had seemed deuced irritated with him when he had first arrived in the library, despite his rescue of her.

Curse it. When he thought of how precariously the ladder had been situated, and when he thought of how she had pitched to the floor...

He stopped himself from contemplating the rest with a shudder, before returning his attention to the meat of the conversation.

"We are only temporarily betrothed," he reminded her, despite the enjoyment he had taken in taunting her with the sham betrothal.

"No one else knows that, however. If we are to be convincing enough to persuade our fellow guests, then we must at least make an attempt at playing the part of besotted betrotheds."

"Besotted?"

Her smile deepened, and he found himself once more transfixed by the gloriousness of her lips. "Yes. Besotted."

Stop looking at her mouth, you stupid arsehole.

He raised a brow. "Our fellow guests are aware of the

reason for our betrothal. That is sufficient. Moreover, no one who knows me will believe I would ever marry *you*. No sense in taking the pretense that far."

The moment the words emerged, he regretted them. Lady Clementine's shoulders sagged, and the corners of her mouth turned down in the most expressive frown he had ever beheld. Had he been too blunt? Too callous?

"Of course," she said quietly.

Two words. The most succinct sentence she had spoken in their admittedly short—and yet somehow far too long—acquaintance. Aside from her horrified shrieks of *bee*, that was. But then, her brevity had been caused by her desire to see the insect in question removed without suffering injury. This time, it seemed to him that *he* had been the cause of the injury.

A strange thing happened.

A pang, in his chest.

Guilt? Surely not. He would have sworn Anna had rendered him incapable of *all* emotions when she had ransacked his future, leaving it to burn to insignificant ash as she married the Marquess of Huntly.

May Huntly's cock rot off, he added as an afterthought.

Lady Clementine said nothing. Her lips, irritatingly plump and prettily pink, *as if she had just been thoroughly kissed*, drew his attention yet again. They were pressed together now in thin, sad lines.

Hell.

"What manner of diminutive?" he found himself asking.

And then promptly wished to kick himself in the arse.

"Something lovely. Something appropriate as well, true to your character and form. Your ears are very large, my lord. I could call you my big-eared rogue, if you like."

He scowled, suppressing the urge to touch his ears, which he was reasonably certain were proportionate and not at all bloody well *large*. "That sounds more like an insult than an endearment."

She blinked. "Oh dear. Does it? What do you think of *my callous coxcomb*?"

She was toying with him, the outrageous woman. Surely she was. She had to be.

Unless?

Mayhap she was a featherwit after all? But nothing in their limited previous interactions had suggested she was. She was either a fool or an incredibly cunning woman.

He was inclined to believe the latter. Her history spoke for itself.

"I think that you had better try again," he ground out, not bothering to spare her feelings after her trickery.

More fluttering of her thick lashes. "My beloved bag of wind? That certainly sounds endearing, and shockingly appropriate..."

He wanted to laugh. And throttle her. And possibly kiss her.

Definitely kiss her.

What the hell was the matter with him? He was not meant to find Lady Clementine Hammond or any of her machinations humorous. *Ye gods*, it was punishment enough that he'd been cursed with the misfortune of being the only other person in proximity when she'd had her altercation with the bee.

And did not that very sentiment say it all? Who else had ever had an *altercation with a damned bee*? No one but the vexing woman before him, he was sure. Who else in the world had managed to have a bee fly up her skirts and sting her inner thigh whilst she was not wearing drawers?

If he'd not been the poor fool who had rushed to her rescue, he would have had quite a laugh over it, he was sure. Mayhap not if the Earl of Rexingham had discovered her.

Mayhap Viscount Wilton. Then again, the viscount was a right proper bore…

"You are looking at me strangely," Lady Clementine said, dragging him from his tumultuous thoughts. "Have I misspoken?"

Had she misspoken?

Damnation. When had she *not* misspoken?

Why could he not shake the feeling that he had been faced with two different versions of Lady Clementine Hammond? And that neither of them was the true Lady Clementine?

She had gone from being closed off and angry with him to ridiculously pleased with the idea of granting him insulting sobriquets. The truth was plain. She was a calculating, cunning minx.

Just as he had thought.

"My beloved bag of wind?" he asked.

"Oh dear." She gave him a new, innocent smile that made his cock rise once more, for there was nothing innocent about this manipulative witch who went about *sans* drawers. "Do you not like it?"

"You may call me Dorset," he repeated his earlier entreaty, more pointed this time. "And I shall call you Lady Clementine."

She pursed her lips. "Hmm."

That mouth of hers.

Something overcame him. Stupidity? Lust? He could not be certain.

Mayhap both, but he was speaking before he could think better of the words tumbling from his own tongue.

"Since we are betrothed, I think it is only fair for us to mark the occasion with a kiss."

"A kiss?" Her smile faltered.

"Just one. Are you amenable?" His head dipped toward

hers, and her scent—jasmine with a hint of something deeper and more exotic—filled his nose.

It was the same scent that had taunted him, lingering in his chamber long after she had gone and then again later, when he had carried her from the gardens to the door of her guest chamber. He did not want to be amused by her, to long to kiss her, to like the way Lady Clementine Hammond smelled. He had no intention of admiring her fortitude.

And yet he was, and he did.

"Yes," she said. "No. That is to say...I suppose. One chaste kiss."

Ah, triumph.

He slid an arm around her waist, drawing her close, anchoring her to him. Her hands settled on his chest like twin, reluctant butterflies. She swallowed, and he followed the movement down the pale skin of her throat. Perversely, he wanted to set his mouth there.

Instead, he lowered his head completely.

At the last moment, she turned, offering him her cheek.

He kissed the high prominence of her bone structure. Her skin was silken. He could not resist trailing a path of kisses. She held still.

All the way to the corner of her lips.

There, he hesitated, drinking in the warmth of her breath as she inhaled, then exhaled her surprise. He wanted her mouth, but he would wait. He remained where he was. Breathing in her breaths. Nuzzling her hair with his nose. And, *Christ help him*, her scent was even more pronounced and delicious here, her tresses luxurious and soft.

She was intoxicating.

He did not mean to find her so.

And yet...she turned her head. Her mouth found his. And the connection...it was sheer *electricity*, just as it had been in his chamber. Not an aberration then as he'd hoped, his reaction to her. If anything, what he felt now was even more intense.

Her lips were warm. Hot, actually. They parted on a gasp.

He took advantage, sliding his tongue into the velvety warmth of her mouth. She tasted of the strawberries she had consumed at breakfast. Sweet and summery and delicious. She hummed into the kiss, and then her tongue moved against his. Her hands slid over his shoulders and linked around his neck. The action pressed her body to his.

Lush breasts crushed into his chest. He clasped the generous curve of her waist, her heat scorching him through her silk gown and underlying layers of civility. He suddenly longed to devour her. Which made no sense. He did not even like her.

But his body certainly liked hers. His lips liked hers beneath them. His body *wanted* hers beneath him, too.

Damnation. They were in the library. Anyone could happen upon them, and then he'd well and truly be forced to marry this harpy. He should stop.

He *would* stop.

Just not yet.

He flattened one palm against her lower back, bringing their bodies into perfect alignment, his aching cock nestled into the softness shielded by the layers of her gown and petticoats. Desire roared inside him, dark and dangerous, threatening to set him aflame. He wanted her. Wanted her and hated her at the same time.

She grasped fistfuls of his tweed coat, holding him tightly to her, and met him kiss for kiss, making the most exquisitely delicious sounds of need low in her throat. God, those sounds. He had to have more of them. To hear those lush, feminine demands for more while he was sliding deep inside her.

His cock was stiffer than a ramrod at the thought of all

her prickly gorgeousness stripped bare, his to tame. If he didn't dislike her so much for her meddlesome ways, he'd be half-inclined to turn their sham betrothal into a true marriage. He could certainly do worse. There was no denying the perverse attraction he felt for her. And her mouth. He couldn't seem to have enough of her full lips, the taste of strawberry on his tongue.

He was ravenous and greedy, sliding his hand up her spine to tangle in the web of dark, sleek hair her lady's maid had captured into an elegant chignon. He wanted it flowing freely. Wanted her tresses falling in waves down her back, over her shoulders. Ambrose's fingers went to work with a mind of their own, plucking hairpins free and plinking them carelessly to the carpet as he ravished her mouth.

Hair draped, silken and heavy and warm, over the back of his hand.

Of all things, it was the unraveling of her hair that brought Lady Clementine back to her senses. She stiffened in his arms, jerking her mouth from his, though not tearing away entirely. With a wide-eyed expression, she gazed up at him wordlessly, lips swollen from his kisses.

"That," she said breathlessly, "was more than one kiss. And decidedly the opposite of chaste."

A reluctant grin pulled at his lips, although he was in no mood for amusement. "There are far more wicked kisses to be had than those. Why, I would venture to call them tepid in comparison to some."

"Tepid," she repeated, brows slamming together. "What other manner are there?"

"So many." He kissed the corner of her lips, then dusted a trail of pecks over her jaw, finding his way to her ear. "Ear kisses, for one."

He brushed his mouth over the elegant whorl, and he didn't miss the little shiver of desire that went through her.

"Hardly wicked," she proclaimed with tempting bravado.

He ran his tongue over the shell. "I wasn't finished yet, darling." Intent upon proving her wrong, he nuzzled the soft skin behind her ear, inhaling deeply the scent of her before licking the soft hollow there.

"Oh," she sighed, clutching his coat in a tighter grip.

She was not as unmoved as she pretended. Determined to prove it to them both, he carried on, grazing his lips over her neck. "There are neck kisses as well." To demonstrate, he opened his mouth and sucked, gratified when she released a breathy moan. He moved lower, trailing his mouth over the full swell of her breasts, trapped behind her stays and bodice. "If you were naked, I'd show you just how wicked kisses can be here." With a finger, he traced the top of one breast, before circling the peak. "And here. I'd suck your nipples into my mouth. Lick them, too."

Her only response was a ragged exhalation of breath.

Good.

This demonstration was proceeding excellently. His cock was throbbing with suppressed need, but it was worth every moment.

He raised his head, holding her gaze. "But my favorite wicked kiss of all is lower still."

She licked her lips, her eyes glazed with desire she couldn't hide from him. "Where?"

Ambrose smiled down at her. "Between your legs."

Another helpless sound of need tumbled from her, and she swayed as if her knees threatened to buckle. Had he shocked her? He hoped he had. But also, he very much wanted to kiss her there. To do far more than that, if he were honest.

"That is positively depraved… You cannot mean…"

His grin deepened. "I can. I do. I'll show you, if you like."

"Dorset!"

It was half scold, half moan.

"At least I'm not your beloved bag of wind," he said. "Perhaps the promise of having your cunny licked is enough to finally tame you."

"Tame me?" Her outrage was as instant as it was fetching. "My…" She trailed off with a shudder, as if she couldn't bear to repeat the word he'd dared to utter, before continuing with her outrage. "Why, you scoundrel, saying such things! Is this naught but a game to you?"

The levity fled him instantly.

He held her stare. "It's no game, Clementine. I want you. I've no inkling why, but I do."

She glared at him. "I like you better when your mouth is otherwise occupied."

"Same, darling."

They stared at each other, at daggers drawn, lust pulsing between them so hotly that it was almost tangible. And then she grabbed his necktie and pulled his mouth down to hers. Their kiss this time was frenzied. He took it as an invitation. And fully intended to show her everything he had promised. As quickly as the desire emerged, his conscience intruded. Perhaps not here. He wasn't sure he was bold enough for such a risk.

But then she sighed into his mouth and sucked on his tongue, and he decided he damned well was. The others were off on some nonsensical walk he'd managed to avoid by going for a morning ride instead. No servant would dare intrude upon them here. The door was firmly closed. They were alone.

She was a bloody fine kisser, Lady Clementine Hammond. He didn't want to know who had taught her the skill, but he suspected he owed that particular gentleman—or gentlemen—his gratitude, followed by a swift fist to the eye. Because she was seducing him. He, the practiced rake who prided himself on engaging in jaded affairs without his icy shell cracking, was unspeakably moved by her kisses alone. By her scent. By her lushness. My God, she was like some sort of deity who had cast a spell over him. One he was helpless to resist.

He was the first to break the seal of their lips, lifting his head to stare down at her, more lovely than any woman—particularly a meddling chit who'd been the bane of his existence—had a right to be. She looked thoroughly kissed and as dazed as he felt. But he wasn't finished yet. A searing rush of possession rose within him, along with need. He wanted to make her come undone. Wanted to pleasure her so well that she forgot every sharp word she had for him. Wanted to hear those moans deepen and feel her quake beneath him with her release.

Ambrose cast a wild glance around and spied an accommodating Grecian couch. Gently, he took Clementine's hand from his necktie and laced their fingers together. Awareness skipped up his arm. Made his cock twitch.

Greedy and impatient, he tugged her toward the nearby furniture.

"What are you doing?" she asked breathlessly, offering no effort to dissuade him from his course.

No protest, nary a hint of stiffness. Instead, she followed him, allowing him to pull her to the green couch.

"Sit, and I'll show you."

She frowned, and he swore he could see her thoughts whirling.

"There mustn't be any of that, darling," he chided, kissing her brow. "Sit."

To his amazement, she obeyed his command, sinking into the upholstery with a lack of elegance he might have found amusing were he not desperate to taste her. He dropped to his knees before her, grateful for the sumptuous carpets.

"Dorset," she breathed, looking bemused. "What are you about?"

"What I promised I would do." He grasped handfuls of voluptuous silk skirts and lifted them higher. "Demonstrating my favorite wicked kiss."

A puff of air left her. He took that as encouragement and bunched her hems up over her knees. He'd seen her limbs before, but that had been in the flurry and haste of trying to rescue her from the dratted bee. Now, he had time to savor the femininity encased in silk, embroidered stockings. The turns of her slender ankles, the curves of her calves, the lacy frills of her garters where her lush thighs began. And by God, she wasn't wearing any drawers again.

He had to swallow hard and gather his composure as he jerked his gaze back to hers. His conscience reminded him this was wrong. Lady Clementine wasn't truly his betrothed. He had no intention of wedding her. And she was a gently bred miss, one who, whilst proficient at kissing, likely possessed no other intimate experience with a man. No, he shouldn't pleasure her. Shouldn't bury his face between her legs.

It was wrong, it was sinful, it was positively perilous for his reputation, a reputation he needed to maintain so he could find a new bride whose dowry would replenish his diminished coffers. He couldn't afford to be caught in a compromising position with Lady Clementine Hammond yet again.

But he fell into her sky-blue gaze, and he saw desire burning in those brilliant depths. Desire that fully matched his own. And he was helpless to resist.

"May I?" he asked, voice hoarse with restrained lust.

Her lips parted. "I don't think…"

Lady Clementine's words trailed away as he glided his

fingertips forward, over smooth, warm skin. "It's best not to think in times such as these."

He fully intended to follow his own advice in that regard, everything else be damned.

She blinked, still looking as dazed as he felt. "Demonstrate away, Dorset. I shall remain impervious."

Dear, wrongheaded Lady Clementine. He would prove how mistaken she was.

Ambrose smiled and, spurred on by wicked intent, for he'd never been one to resist a challenge, pressed a kiss to her inner knee. "We'll see about that."

"I'm quite unmoved," the minx announced from above.

He trailed his tongue along her inner thigh in response, getting closer to his prize. "How about now?"

"No change," she said breathlessly.

Ha! He wrestled with her layers, shoving them higher and revealing more glorious bare skin. More delicious temptation. For such an irritating woman, she certainly was delightfully appealing. It was unfair.

"Hold up your skirts for me, darling," he told her.

Dainty, pale fingers grasped her hems, obliging him again.

"Higher," he ordered.

"Do hurry, Dorset. I'm growing bored."

The thickness in her voice couldn't be denied. Oh, he was going to enjoy this even more than he had originally supposed.

"If you insist," he said lightly, releasing his hold on her gown so that he could touch her freely, skimming his palms up to her hips.

God, she was soft. Reverently, he guided her legs apart, noting the reddened patch where she'd suffered the bee sting and taking care to avoid it. She opened for him, and he was treated to a perfect view of glistening, feminine flesh. Her breath caught. Or maybe it was his. He drew nearer, his head dipping, the sweet, musky scent of her invading his senses a potent lure.

Gently, he brushed his lips over the pouting bud at the top of her sex.

There was no question who the gasp above him belonged to.

"Still bored?" he had the presence of mind to ask.

She must have lost her hold on her gown, for it slipped, heavy layers draping over his head and enveloping him in darkness. Her only response was a small pant from somewhere above, muffled by the sea of silk and underskirts surrounding him. He licked her then, giving in to the base urge to know the taste of her on his tongue.

Musk and sweetness, mysteries and Clementine. Damn the woman. He might have known she would be the most mouthwatering delicacy he'd ever had.

Tentatively, he turned himself to his task—making her weak with lust until she had no choice but to admit defeat and come all over his face like the wicked wanton he knew she secretly was. The very notion of it made his cock achingly hard. But that determined devil would have to remain trapped in his trousers and begging for a release he'd only be able to achieve later, in the privacy of his own chamber. Strangely, the anticipation and denial only heightened his desire.

He took his time, lavishing long, lingering licks up and down her seam before finding her pearl and flicking over it. Her hips bucked, and he heard her swift inhalation. She liked that. He would have further needled her about her feigned boredom, but he hadn't the inclination to remove his mouth from her sweet cunny.

Ambrose devoured her, showing no mercy. In this little battle of theirs, he would not relent until he had her shuddering and crying out beneath him. He whorled his tongue over her, licked and sucked.

As if from afar, he heard her long, low moan. Her body was tensing beneath him, undulating against the relentless pressure of his mouth, chasing what he suspected she didn't even know she wanted.

But he would give it to her. He caressed her inner thigh, careful to avoid her bee sting, and found his way to her center. One slow swipe up her seam and he was almost lost himself. She was so hot and slick, soft and satiny and beckoning with forbidden welcome. He circled her entrance, finding it with ease, and she gasped again, hips arching, skirts falling until he was completely hidden beneath a curtain of feminine fabric. There had never been a better place to be.

He surrendered to the need to pleasure her, to possess her. He sank a finger inside, her cunny instantly tightening on him as he licked and sucked her into a wild frenzy. She felt so good. Like heaven, really, and he thought he might gladly throw himself into the fire of Hades for an eternity just for the opportunity to slide inside her heat and fuck her until they were both spent and sated.

But no, he couldn't do either of those things. To truly make love to her would be sheer and utter folly. This was not a true betrothal, but a falsehood designed to fool their fellow guests and save their reputations. However, it didn't feel much like a sham with his face buried between her lush thighs and his finger deep inside her. She was close. He could feel it, and by God, he wasn't far himself.

Ambrose suckled her pearl and worked in and out of her, penetrating with greater devotion and intent, curling his finger to find the place he knew would drive her mad, and then she was there.

Clementine cried out.

Almost a scream.

It was a high, helpless cry of pure, unadulterated release. Her sweet cunny clamped down on his finger, body jerking forward, quivering and trembling as she pulsed around him, coming undone so beautifully. He licked her gently, savoring the taste of her, the way she responded, her unabashed embracing of her own innate sensuality.

And then he reluctantly emerged from beneath her skirts, licking her juices from his lips, flipping her hems back into place as he found her flushed and partially collapsed on the couch. It had, he realized grimly, been the singularly most erotic moment of his life. Pity it had been with a woman he despised for her meddling in his private affairs and those of others. Why couldn't it have been anyone other than her?

Trying to quell his rampaging cockstand, he met her passion-glazed stare. "I trust I've successfully banished your *ennui*, Lady Clementine."

It was a desperately rude thing to say to a lady he'd just brought to her peak. And not just that, but an unwed lady who'd been far more innocent when she'd entered the library than she'd be when she left it. He deserved a slap for it.

But Lady Clementine straightened as if a pail of cold water had just been upended on her, her spine ramrod stiff. "It was passable," she said coolly.

Breathlessly.

She was lying. They both knew it. But he would allow her to cling to her pride.

For now.

Ambrose drew to his feet, offering her a mocking bow. "Perhaps I'll have to practice with another and improve my craft," he drawled, although he had no intention to do so. The only woman who had drawn his interest at this bloody house party was—blast it—*her*. "I'll leave you to your books."

Without waiting for her response, he fled the library, his

strides eating up the distance between himself and the privacy of his chamber. Once inside, he slammed the door, unable to make it another step before opening the fall of his trousers and taking his cock in hand. He gripped his shaft hard, and all it took was three strokes before he came with almost violent abandon, the decadent taste of Lady Clementine still on his tongue.

He ought to have been ashamed. If he'd been a gentleman, he likely would have been. But as the intense tide of passion gradually ebbed and he came to his senses, leaning against the wall with his heart hammering in his chest, Ambrose knew nary a single regret.

CHAPTER 7

*C*lementine took her aim with care and released the arrow. It sailed through the air and landed with precision on the target, directly in the center where she had intended.

"Excellent shot, Tiny," Charity congratulated her, clapping her hands.

"I was pretending it was Lord Dorset," she announced.

That was a lie, of course.

She would never do the marquess violence. Quite the opposite, in fact, and much to her dismay. Ever since the shocking, wicked, wonderful incident in the library, all she could do was think about him. And long for more.

Curse the man.

He had her quite out of sorts.

Her answer for that had been simple: avoidance. If he wasn't within reach, he couldn't tempt her. Or touch her. Or kiss her…

She ruthlessly quelled the pang of disappointment at the thought of no more clever, practiced seductions from the Marquess of Dorset. He wasn't for her, she reminded herself firmly. No man was. She'd had her heart crushed once, and that had been more than enough.

"But he is your betrothed," Lady Edith reminded her, plucking an arrow from the quiver at her own station and readying her bow.

Clementine sighed. "I've already told you that he isn't."

"Perhaps someone ought to tell Dorset that," Vivi added from her nearby station. "He seems quite convinced otherwise."

"My betrothal is temporary," she told her friend in a low voice, too aware of their fellow guests presiding over the afternoon's entertainment from the chairs set up at the end of the archery range.

She hadn't had the opportunity to speak with Vivi alone now that the house party was truly underway and Sherborne Manor had become inundated with guests. Of course, Vivi also seemed quite happily occupied by her husband. Another pang hit Clementine then. An unworthy one. No, she was not envious of the love her dear friend shared with Bradford. She didn't want a husband. She was perfectly content to remain a spinster forever.

To the devil with all men. They were nothing but inconstant sinners intent upon luring innocent ladies into the seedy spider web of debauchery.

"Temporary?" Vivi's brows rose. "I'll admit, I have been wondering, but we haven't had the opportunity for a moment alone. You never said a word about Dorset before his arrival."

With a sigh, Clementine settled her bow in her station. "That is because I never thought about Dorset before his arrival."

Or before those heated kisses they'd shared. In his chamber. In the library.

She wished she had a fan to cool her suddenly heated face, but there were none about.

Vivi cocked her head at Clementine, regarding her with a gaze that saw far too much. "But you think about him now."

It was impossible not to think about the wretched man. He inhabited all her thoughts. Him and his mouth that knew how to kiss, and his wicked tongue, and his skilled fingers. Sweet heavens, she mustn't allow her mind to continue straying to such a dangerous place. She'd go up in flames.

"I think about him as much as I must, given his ridiculous and erroneous announcement," she corrected with as much dignity as she could muster. "The man is vexing. And maddening. And infuriating. And vexing."

"You called him vexing twice," Lady Edith pointed out, rather unhelpfully.

Clementine turned to her new friend with a pointed glare. "That is because he is doubly vexing. More vexing than anyone else in my acquaintance."

Lady Edith blinked behind her spectacles. "That is vexing indeed."

Clementine didn't know the other woman well enough to know if she was being mocked. She rather suspected Lady Edith possessed a great deal more backbone than Clementine had previously realized.

"Just how vexing is he?" Charity asked slyly. "Has he seduced you, Tiny? Please say he has."

Yes. Good heavens. Yes, he had, indeed. But she would perish of mortification before she revealed such a fall from grace to her friends in the midst of the house party, surrounded by fellow guests.

"Charity!" she exclaimed. "Do lower your voice, if you please. I've no wish to start a scandal, and Lady Featherstone's ears are sharper than a blade." She turned to Lady Edith with a wince, belatedly realizing she'd just disparaged her new friend's mother. "Apologies, my lady, for any offense."

"None taken," Lady Edith assured her with a small smile. "*Maman's* reputation quite proceeds her."

"You haven't answered my question," Charity pointed out. "Has Dorset—"

"Charity," she interrupted in a tone of warning.

"Escorted you through the gardens?" Charity finished with an exaggerated look of wide-eyed innocence. "It was a simple enough question. No need to be cross with me."

"Of course he hasn't *escorted me through the gardens*," she said with feeling.

A lie, of course. If they were calling seduction a walk through the gardens, then Dorset most certainly had thoroughly, and without compunction, *waltzed* her through the gardens.

"Pity," Charity said, her eyes narrowing in a considering fashion, as if she did not entirely believe Clementine. "His reputation suggests he would make the experience quite enjoyable."

Yes, it did. And yes, he had—she couldn't lie to herself about that. Every moment with Dorset in the library had been most enjoyable. His chamber as well. Deliciously, wrongly enjoyable. And that was precisely why she intended to keep the man far, far away from her for the remainder of the house party. One fortnight. She could certainly manage to keep her distance for a paltry two weeks.

Couldn't she?

"Has anyone escorted *you* through the gardens, my dear?" Clementine demanded of her friend.

Charity chuckled, devilish merriment gleaming in her eyes. "Not yet, but the house party has only just begun. There's time aplenty for garden exploration."

"Saints preserve us," murmured Lady Edith, looking rather bemused by their frank conversation.

"Don't forget the true reason this house party has been convened," Vivi reminded them with an arch look. "The Lady's Suffrage Society is in dire need of all the support we can rouse for our new petition to the House of Lords."

"How could we forget?" Charity asked, taking aim and sending an arrow sailing into the target with jaunty ease. "*Gardening* is lovely, but nothing is more important than getting the vote."

Gardening, indeed. Charity was a wild hellion, and it was a miracle she'd managed to maintain her reputation with all the scrapes she'd managed to find herself in, thanks to her boisterous, outspoken nature. She was a true original.

"Speaking of the cause, I would like to join you," Lady Edith said firmly then, surprising them all.

"This is wonderful news!" Vivi exclaimed, grinning as she broke into a little delighted clap.

"What will your mother think?" Clementine couldn't help asking.

"I don't care," Lady Edith announced, chin going up in stubborn defiance.

"Huzzah for that," Vivi said approvingly. "I'll speak with Lady Featherstone if you think it would help smooth the way."

"I think I'd like to tell her myself," Lady Edith said.

"Brave girl," Charity applauded. "I'm proud of you, my dear."

Yes, Clementine reminded herself sternly. Their cause was of the utmost importance. Far more than the fleeting pleasures to be had from a rakehell's lips.

And tongue.

And, heaven help her, *teeth*.

Clementine lifted her bow and took aim, pretending it

was Dorset's beautiful, smiling visage in the midst of the target. Her arrow arced through the air and found its mark with a solid *thwack*.

∽

AMBROSE WAS hell-bent upon driving the memory of Lady Clementine's soaked, hot cunny from his mind. An impossible feat, for he'd been able to think of little else ever since he'd pleasured her in the library the day before.

Banishing all recognition of her—purging her from his thoughts altogether—continued to be his aim. However, as he indulged in a game of billiards with fellow house party guest Viscount Wilton, he could not deny that the maddening lady in question was as stubborn in her domination of his mind as she was in every other aspect of life.

Curse the meddlesome female.

"I say, Dorset. You are markedly Friday-faced for a chap who is winning this particular game of billiards," Wilton observed, his ever-present frown sterner and harsher than ever.

The viscount was a frigid fellow, though pleasant enough to engage in a friendly diversion.

As long as Ambrose had some spirits in hand. Where *was* the goddamn brandy? He found himself desperately in need of another glass.

"One might issue the same remark to you, Wilton," he pointed out, perhaps unkindly.

He took aim and sent his cue ball neatly into the viscount's and the object ball, scoring another point.

"You are despicably good at billiards, and I dislike losing," the viscount responded, taking his turn and scoring a point of his own. "Surely that is reason enough."

He supposed. Wilton was quite skilled at billiards, but

Ambrose had yet to meet a billiards player he could not trounce. "Losing is dreadful."

He'd been blessed with the devil's own luck his entire life. There had been very few instances when he had lost any game or sport, from *vingt-et-un* to cricket to football. His biggest loss of all had been Lady Anna.

And he must not allow himself to forget the reason for that loss. She had a name—Lady Clementine Hammond. Unfortunately, because his body was a hateful traitor, she also made his cock hard.

Deuced unfortunate timing. The woman was nowhere near him. He was playing billiards with Wilton. Far away from her, for Chrissakes. Irritated with himself, he took aim and hit the cue with too much force. It landed just wide of the viscount's ball.

"I would think a newly betrothed man would be in finer spirits," Wilton said, taking aim and scoring once more.

Blast on two counts. The viscount was nearly tying him now, and he had also brought up Ambrose's own personal Gorgon.

"I wear my excitement on the inside," he drawled, before sending his cue flying once more.

And missing the object ball and Wilton's yet again.

"I must admit, I'm hoping to procure myself a betrothed before the house party's end," Wilton said. "Have you any advice, having snared Lady Clementine so swiftly?"

The viscount earned another point.

Tied now. Ambrose was bloody well in danger of losing. And in more ways than one.

"Get caught with your hands under the lady's skirts," he said wryly, though he knew he ought not.

The less mentioning of the scandal, the better. If he reminded others of his ignominious scene with the meddlesome Lady Clementine, how the hell was he going to throw her over at the end of the damned house party?

With ease and with relish, of course. Who the hell cared if he caused a scandal? No amount of wagging tongues could persuade him to marry her. There were other women in society with far larger dowries than hers.

"I had heard some rumbling, but surely you jest." Wilton was staring at him, looking dismayed.

He sighed, for he knew the viscount was a curmudgeonly stickler, but he had forgotten the extent of it. Could a man not simply have a drink and play a game of billiards and relax his guard?

"I wish I were jesting," he muttered. "Unfortunately for Lady Clementine, a bee decided to find its way under her gown in…er, the moment I was confessing my undying love to her."

Those last words stuck in his throat like a fish bone, for no man believed in love less than Ambrose.

"Ah, I begin to understand." The viscount's expression had gone as stiff as his posture. "I am not seeking a love match. My felicitations to you."

Neither am I, old chap, he wanted to say.

But he forced himself to recall that Wilton was not his friend, but an acquaintance. And one whose rigid sense of propriety would likely find offense in the dismal truth.

"Thank you," he said grimly as he took his next shot.

"What do you know of Lady Charity Manners?" Wilton asked.

The blonde beauty had a bold reputation. Rumor had it that she had posed for a famed portrait of Venus that had been shown at the Grosvenor Gallery the year before. It would not have been particularly shocking had not the Venus in question been nude.

Dorset studied the viscount, wondering if he had failed to

hear the rumors. "Scarcely anything," he lied brightly, deciding that if Wilton had not, there was no need to be the bearer of ill tidings.

"What of Lady Edith?" the viscount asked next.

The red-haired, bespectacled lady in question seemed scholarly and kind. "She is greatly interested in the ruins here at Sherborne Manor," he offered.

"Miss Lucy and Miss Madeline Chartrand?"

Damnation. The man truly *was* interested in finding himself a wife.

Dorset suppressed a shudder as he pondered the question. "They are both lovely. However, unless I miss my guess, the Earl of Rexingham has already captured Miss Lucy's interest. Miss Madeline appears unattached. She has an impressive fortune—an American dollar princess, as they say. If you're in need of replenishing the familial coffers, she is the lady you ought to woo."

Actually, now that he thought upon it, Miss Madeline Chartrand was the lady Ambrose himself ought to be wooing. Her father's immense wealth would do wonders to aid Ambrose in repairing his crumbling estates. Pity he wasn't interested in her. Not in the slightest.

The viscount's frown turned more severe. "My familial coffers are hardly empty."

What haughty pride.

Ambrose shrugged. "I never meant to suggest they were, old chap. My intent was to help you with your aim."

It was his turn, so he hit the cue, once more narrowly avoiding striking the object ball.

Wilton regarded him with the first sign of amusement he had displayed thus far. "It would appear that of the two of us, you are the one more in need of help with his aim."

Well, damn it all. The viscount was right, and in more than one way.

CHAPTER 8

The moon shone high overhead, casting the extensive gardens of Sherborne Manor in an ethereal silver glow. The Yorkshire air was cooler than the day had been, tinged with the sweetness of the gardens in bloom. On the air tonight: sweet peas blending with the perfume of Vivi's prized rose collection. But the stillness and beauty of the garden at night was somewhat lost upon Clementine as she made her way along the gravel path for the first time since her unfortunate bee sting incident.

The evening's entertainment was musical in nature, but despite her need for distraction, Clementine had slipped from the crowded music room. She could not seem to quell the rising sense of unease that had been haunting her since long before her arrival at Sherborne Manor.

In truth, it had been haunting her ever since…

Walter.

One name, one man, and yet years later, the memory of their ill-fated courtship still had the ability to affect her. But mayhap it was the notion of being betrothed once more— regardless of the legitimacy of the betrothal—that had spurred her melancholy more than ever this evening. Once, she had been desperately in love, or so she'd thought, happily on her way to becoming the Countess of Ormond, and then, her future had been ruthlessly ripped from her grasp.

Because Walter had never had any intention of marrying her. He had toyed with her. Kissed her in hidden alcoves. Whispered pretty words of love. But then he'd eloped with Miss Beatrice Stanhope, whose family fortune had rivaled that of Croesus himself, and he'd forgotten her very existence.

She sighed again at her own foolishness, the burning shame that had yet to leave her, and wandered along the meandering path, casting her eyes to the gossamer clouds and twinkling stars.

"Looking for me, beloved?"

The unexpected voice, a deep and decadent rumble that was already far more familiar than it ought to be, gave her such a start that she made a most humiliating squealing sound. Rather akin to a frightened mouse, she expected. One who was being stalked by a cat about to pounce.

For there, in the milky moonlight, appeared none other than the tall, handsome Marquess of Dorset strolling about a tall grouping of roses.

She pressed a hand to her furiously pounding heart and glared at Dorset through the space separating them. "What are you doing in the gardens?"

"You disappeared into the night. I merely wished to make certain you were well—and that there weren't any angry bees in the vicinity." He sauntered toward her, and that was when she detected the faint glow in his hand.

The undeniable scent of tobacco reached her, cloaking the floral perfume of the blossoms. He was smoking a cigar in the gardens, when he was meant to have been listening to Miss Hortense Sinclair singing whilst Lady Eleanor Grant played the piano. Truly, she could not blame him, for Miss Sinclair was a wretched singer.

"I am well enough," she said cooly, not wanting to allow him to see her vulnerability.

"You seem melancholy," he countered. "Surely something is amiss for you to flee our hostess's planned entertainments for the evening. Why not share what is troubling you? I am, after all, your future husband and savior in relation to all bees."

Clementine might have smiled were she not so thoroughly reminded of all the devastating reasons she must never trust another libertine. Regardless of how handsome they were or how charming and persuasive.

"You needn't concern yourself with my welfare," she said. "Pray, carry on with your cigar and your solitude. I'll return to the party."

But when she attempted to pass him on the gravel path, he halted her with a gentle hand on her arm. "Wait, my dear." He flicked his cigar into a nearby fountain. "Won't you tell me what is bothering you? Seeing your frowning countenance makes me peevish. Has someone upset you? I'll challenge them to a duel."

He was being silly. Almost sweet. She didn't dare trust him.

"You know very well that no one fights duels any longer, and furthermore, nothing is amiss," she told him. "Truly you ought not to go about tossing your cigars in the Duchess of Bradford's garden fountain. Heaven forbid you should clog it. She's just had the entire affair restored."

Vivi was quite proud of her efforts. The fountain with its nude cherubs had been something of a source of amusement for the two of them when Clementine had first arrived at Sherborne Manor. But she wouldn't lie, chastising the marquess was a welcome distraction. She did not need to think of Walter when she was taking Dorset to task.

"Eh, I am certain I'm not the first gentleman to toss his cigar into the fountain. I would wager Tildon Court upon it."

"Your family seat?" she guessed, for she did not make a habit of remembering the estates and the lords who owned them.

"It is," he confirmed, lingering near enough that his scent, musky and masculine beneath the lingering smell of the cigar smoke, and strangely alluring, reached her.

"Tell me about it," she said, seeking distraction even as she knew she ought to return to the safety of the music room.

The less time she spent in Dorset's presence, the better. And yet…

Here, she remained. Intrigued. Drawn to him somehow on a deeper level she could not fathom. It was unexpected. Inexplicable, too. It was reckless and thoroughly unwise. Had she not learned her lesson? Did she not know what dreadful perils awaited every lady who succumbed to the wiles of a rake? Of course she did.

"On one condition."

With only the moon for illumination, she was not certain she could accurately read the marquess's expression. "Do not ask me for more kisses," she warned and then bit her lip.

What a ninny she was. Why had she mentioned kissing to him? Why was she thinking of how she had felt in the library, when he'd been kissing her everywhere before slipping beneath her skirts? And why was she thinking about his mouth on her there, of how wondrous it had been, that dark and dangerous introduction to a passion she'd never previously imagined?

"If it is another wicked kiss you want, you need only say so, my beloved—"

"It is not," she hastened to add, interrupting him sternly before she went up in flames.

He cocked his head, considering her in the moonlight, and she found herself wondering what it was he saw. "You make me doubt my prowess with such a hasty and succinct refusal, darling."

His nonchalance was more bitter proof of precisely what he was, if she hadn't been certain from his reputation and his behavior in the library. The Marquess of Dorset was a rakehell.

"I suppose that is why you truly followed me out into the gardens," she said bitterly. "Hoping for another illicit tryst like the rest of your brethren?"

He straightened. "The rest of my brethren?"

"Rakes," she bit out. "Libertines. Scoundrels. For that is what you are, is it not, Lord Dorset? No gentleman would have behaved as you did yesterday in the library."

"I never claimed to be a gentleman." He flashed her a smile that revealed even, white teeth gleaming in the silvery light. "Far from it, in fact. Everyone knows proper gentlemen are bloody boring."

She stared at him, wishing she didn't take note of the fine figure he cut in the darkness, his broad shoulders, tall form, his long, lean legs. He was breathtaking in an otherworldly sense in this dearth of sun.

"I like proper gentlemen," she blurted.

"But you also like *me*," he countered lightly.

And not without merit.

"I don't like you, Dorset." It felt like a lie. The troublesome rogue was beginning to grow on her, much to her horror.

His grin deepened. "You like what I do to you."

"I suspect anyone would."

"Shall I test your hypothesis?" He moved suddenly,

skirting her on the narrow path. "I'll find another willing lady and report back with her response."

Her hand shot out of its own accord, staying him. "No."

He paused, casting her a curious glance that somehow made her feel quite hot everywhere, but particularly in that place he had so thoroughly explored the day before. "No?"

She cleared her throat. "Leave the other ladies in peace."

"Because you would prefer to keep me to yourself, darling?" He pressed a hand over his heart. "I'm touched."

She released her hold on his coat sleeve as if it burned her. "Hardly. What you do and with whom is of no concern to me. Having been scorned by a rake in the past, I'm the last woman in the world who would lay claim to one."

"Ah, I begin to understand," he said softly, and with a tenderness that suggested he did, indeed.

She wished she'd not spoken so freely.

"I'm sure you don't," she said, struggling to keep old emotion and bitterness from her voice. "If you'll excuse me, my lord, I truly must return to the music room before I'm missed."

"Nonsense." Sounding grim, Dorset took her hands in his. "Come."

Neither of them wore gloves, Clementine having abandoned hers on a stone wall when she had first entered the gardens, and Dorset's likely secreted in a pocket. His skin was warm, his fingers long and strong and somehow reassuring even as she didn't wish for them to be. He tugged, taking control of the moment.

And for some perverse reason, she allowed it, following him to a nearby bench. The moment was oddly reminiscent of the last time they had found themselves seemingly alone in the gardens. However, on this occasion, there was no bee, no calamity, no nearby hostess and fellow guests to hear her frantic shrieks and come in search of her.

"Sit," he ordered, but there was an unusual edge of kindness to his words that made her obey.

Her knees had turned mutinous anyway. They gave out. Her rump, insufficiently padded by the underpinnings of her gown, landed hard upon the stone bench. She winced.

"What is the matter?" he asked. "Surely not another bee? I thought the blighters slept in the darkness."

Had she made a sound of discomfort, or was he merely that attuned to her? Clementine could not be certain. Either way, his sudden concern was…confusing. And he was still holding her hands in his as he seated himself at her side.

Strangely, she did not want to relinquish either her hold on him or his on her.

He felt so very real and alive, so vital and necessary. It was a trick of the night, a foolish imagining brought on by her confused emotions. And yet, she could not seem to let go.

"Not a bee," she managed to say. "I was merely shocked by my landing upon the stone bench. It was rather graceless."

"You've a sore rump, in other words. Shall I kiss it to make it better?"

The man was dreadful. But he was teasing her, and despite herself, she was charmed.

Her cheeks went hot. But she didn't release her hold on his hand. Their fingers were interlaced now, and it was strangely comforting. "You must not speak of my rump, Lord Dorset."

"Why? I daresay it is a fine one indeed."

"You are a ridiculous man."

"I'm your ridiculous betrothed," he corrected, tracing soft circles on her palm with his thumb. "The rake who scorned you in the past, who was he?"

She did not want to talk about Walter any longer, and yet, she also very much wanted to unburden herself. "It doesn't matter who he is. He has long since married another for her fortune and carried on with his life. And now, he's making a fool of his wife as well."

The last she'd heard, Walter's marriage had not hindered his amorous conquests in the slightest. Not surprising, although Clementine did pity his poor countess.

"It matters to me," he countered. "If I'm to blacken a man's eye for breaking my betrothed's heart, I need to know his name first."

"Dorset, you're not going to blacken anyone's eye," she protested, although something inside her warmed at the notion of him charging to her defense.

Walter possessed a far slighter form than the marquess. She had no doubt Dorset would trounce him in a fight.

"Ambrose."

She blinked. "I beg your pardon?"

"My given name. It is Ambrose. Formality between the two of us seems fruitless in the darkness, does it not?"

She could not argue. What was it about the night that made her somehow more inclined to confide in him? He seemed almost like—dare she think it—another friend.

Albeit, a friend she wanted to kiss.

No. She must stop all such wayward thoughts. Banish them to the ethereal clouds above and then beyond.

"It does," she agreed with great reluctance.

Because the recollection of his mouth on her body was a burning, decadent memory that threatened to undo all her good intentions.

"Ambrose, then." He gave her fingers another squeeze and leaned his shoulder into hers. "Deuced better than *my beloved bag of wind*, would you not agree?"

She found herself chuckling, grateful for his kindness. "But I thought I was to call you Dorset. Because it is your name."

How could a shoulder pressed against hers feel as intimate as a kiss? She could not say. And yet, it did. She was at once aware of his searing warmth, his inherent strength. He was much larger than she was, and yet she did not feel overwhelmed by his height or his masculine form. Quite the opposite, in fact.

He leaned into her some more, his head canted in her direction. "I shall make an exception for you."

His sudden tenderness toward her made a strange, fluttery sensation burst to life in her stomach. She was not sure she liked it.

Or him.

Yes, I do. At least, I like his mouth quite well.

"Stop that," she muttered to herself.

"Stop what?" he asked.

Oh dear. She was chastising herself aloud now. Could her mortification be any more complete?

"Pitying me," she said.

"I do not pity you, Clementine."

She took note of the familiarity in his tone, in his foregoing of the honorific. "Then why are you being so nice to me?"

"Was I not nice to you before this evening?" His voice sounded darkly amused. "I rescued you from a bee sting and a fall in the library."

So he had. But that had been different. *He* had been different than he was now. More distant, and not just in terms of physical proximity. Was it the darkness or her admission that had rendered him less bitter, no longer as harsh as he had been before?

"You did not save me from the sting," she pointed out, leaning into him before she could think better of the action, their shoulders and elbows rubbing together.

"I suppose not. Merely from walking after you suffered from the unfortunate injury. How is the sting feeling?"

More concern for her welfare from the Marquess of Dorset?

"It no longer hurts." Instead, it itched rather dreadfully. But she was not going to tell him that.

"I reckon it is deuced itchy," he said, as if reading her thoughts.

Her cheeks went hot, and she was grateful for the darkness of the night that would keep him from seeing her reaction. "Not at all."

"Hmm. Does your lady's maid not have some cream or potion to aid you?"

"No," she admitted quietly. "She does not."

"About a year ago when I was in the countryside, I was riding my mare when we riled a wasp's nest. The devils were overzealous with their stinging. My valet whipped up a concoction that eased my discomfort. I shall check with him for you."

This, too, was kind of him. She was going to suggest it was improper for him to make inquiries on her behalf, particularly when the wound in question possessed such intimate placement.

But when she opened her mouth, two words emerged instead. "Thank you."

His thumb, which had been tracing circles on her palm all this time, ventured to her inner wrist. A frisson went through her. A new sense of heightened awareness blossomed.

"May I ask you a question?" she asked him, trying to ignore the flurry of sensations.

"We shall make a bargain. You may ask me a question, and I may ask you one in return."

She studied him through the moonlight, taking note of the wide angle of his jaw, the blade of his nose. His eyes sparkled in the gossamer illumination. Handsome. Even in the shadows, he was so very attractive. She could not deny it any more than she could pretend there was not a fervent hunger glowing within her whenever she was near to this man.

Regardless of how much she did not wish to feel it.

Dorset is a dreadful rake, she reminded herself. *Not to be trusted.*

"I am not certain I should agree to such an arrangement," she told him warily.

∽

CLEMENTINE WAS WISE NOT to trust the wisdom of such a bargain with him.

But then, he had already warned her that he was no gentleman.

"The bargain I suggested is only fair," he told her, struggling to keep the growing need to seize her mouth with his once more at bay. "If you want my answer, I require yours."

"Fair enough." The glow of the moonlight illuminated the bright white of her teeth nibbling on her lower lip.

Damn.

His cock twitched.

"What was your question?" he ground out.

"The Marchioness of Huntly," she said softly.

Lady Anna's title and the fact that she was another man's wife still felt like an unwelcome surprise, for he'd been so very certain she would wed him and solve all his financial woes. He'd spent a great deal of time wooing her, and he'd never lost when it came to matters of the fairer sex. Until Lady Anna. He would do well to remember the tempting woman before him was the cause of it.

He tensed. "That is not a question but a name."

"Did you love her?"

The question was unwanted, for no response he could give would present him in a beneficial light. He realized belatedly that he was still holding her hand, their fingers laced, his thumb upon the velvet skin of her inner wrist. He could not be certain if he wanted to release his hold or keep touching her.

Keep touching her, whispered a wicked voice within.

"Perhaps I should not have asked."

"No," he bit out with more force than necessary. "You should not have done."

But he was still holding her, somehow reluctant to sever the connection between them, however tenuous, however unlikely.

"Forgive me." She tugged her hand from his and rose from the bench, slipping further into the night.

He rose, following her, swallowing more than one flavor of regret. "Clementine."

She spun about in a swirl of dark skirts. Because he had been watching her earlier through dinner, he knew they were lush, vibrant-red silk rather than the almost-ebony they appeared in the absence of shimmering gas lamps.

"You blame me for what happened," she said.

It was not a question.

He did not bother with pretense. "Should I not?"

"You think poorly of me."

Once again, her words were not query but statement. He found himself pondering them. Did he? It was undeniable that when he had arrived at the house party, he had. She was a meddler, the reason Anna had been forced to marry Huntly.

But now...

What the devil was wrong with him?

Now, the lines were blurring, becoming indistinct. Right and wrong no longer seemed finite. And the blame he had cast upon her did not seem entirely deserving. She was not a heartless wretch as he had once supposed. She had a sharp wit, Lady Clementine Hammond. She met him verbal thrust for parry.

For some reason, he very much did not want her to disappear deeper into the gardens thinking he believed the worst of her or that she believed the worst of him. Very well. The reason was because he...

Egads.

He cared about Lady Clementine Hammond's opinion.

Likely because of the way his body reacted to hers, he reasoned. Her kisses. The wine he had drunk at dinner. The knock he had taken to the head in the wee hours of the morning when he had shifted too near to the headboard in his sleep... There had to be an explanation that made sense.

Somehow, he could find none.

"I don't think poorly of you," he admitted with great reluctance.

"Oh?" Her tone was cool, her posture, even in the sprightly silver gilt of the moon, defensive.

It was a fair question. Still, before the last few days, he had been persuaded that he did not like her at all. That she was a dreadful person. A purveyor of misery.

Now?

He swallowed. "I do not," he repeated. "However, you asked your question, and now I must have my turn. Why did you make certain to catch Lady Anna and Huntly alone?"

She stilled. "Our bargain was a question and an answer for the same."

He supposed he had not answered her question. And the reason for that was plain.

"I'm not certain I could say that I was in love with her now," he admitted. "At the time, I was persuaded there was the capacity for something more between us. We possessed a certain…accord. And then another party intervened, changing the prescribed course."

She had intervened, in more ways than one.

Though he kept that bit to himself.

Because what if the intervention had been for the best?

Hell. He did not want to contemplate the possibility, and yet how could he deny it? When he was standing here in the gardens, surrounded by the charmed moonlight, the sweet scent on the air a combination of Clementine and the Duchess of Bradford's rosebushes in bloom, Lady Anna was far from his mind.

Lady Clementine nodded. "Fair enough. Such matches are common enough in our set, even if loathsome. I suppose I must give you your answer now. It is not as simple as one might suppose. I am more than aware of my reputation. But the matches I have made…they have never been out of spite. When I was betrayed…"

The bastard who had dared to hurt her again. *Bloody hell.*

He ground his molars, forcing himself to be the gentleman he decidedly was not and keep from demanding she give him the scoundrel's name. "Go on."

"I wanted to make others happy, although I knew I could not be." Her quiet words were almost lost in the hush of the night.

But he heard them. He heard *her*. And for the first time, he thought he understood Lady Clementine Hammond.

All this time, he had believed her a vicious, cunning snake, and in truth, she had been a broken, wounded soul. One who believed, however wrongly, that catching others in compromising positions, and leading them to their nuptials, was doing them a favor.

"How many couples?" he asked, knowing he need not elaborate.

"Half a dozen or more." She raised her chin. "I was hardly

keeping count. But when the truth was so plain for me to see...I suppose it became something of an obsession for me. A distraction. If I was facilitating the happiness of others, I did not have to fret over the lack of happiness in my own life. It made me feel...necessary, I suppose. They have all thanked me for my intervention."

The jagged pieces inside him seemed somehow less sharp. "Even Lady Anna?"

"Yes." Her voice was soft and tinged with sympathy. "Even her. She and Huntly are a love match."

He had not spoken to Anna since she had tearfully thrown him over in favor of the marquess. Their interactions had been limited to being guests at the same social events, but their paths had not directly crossed, thanks to Dorset's efforts to avoid her.

The news that Anna was happy with Huntly was surprising. But strangely, the knowledge did not fill him with pain or bitterness. Instead, he found himself distracted by the woman at his side, her scent filling him with yearning. Her delectable curves tempting his fingers to learn all the dips and swells.

"You are being quiet," she observed.

So he was. "It never occurred to me to ask her whether or not she was content," he admitted, recognizing his own conceit. "The day she threw me over was the last I ever spoke to her."

She had sent him a handful of letters initially. He had tossed each one into the fire without reading a word.

Now, he wondered what she had written. An explanation? An apology? He supposed it hardly mattered. The past was where it belonged.

"It was not my intention to catch her alone with the Marquess of Huntly," Clementine offered, her gaze on him, seeking through the moonbeams.

What did she see? A jaded rake who had somehow found himself at the mercy of a matchmaking lady? A rogue who no longer believed himself capable of caring and yet was nonetheless experiencing a disturbing feeling of affinity for the last woman at the house party he ought?

Blast. Why did he want to kiss her again? To have her in his arms, to unwrap her like the most delicious gift, and to sink inside her lush heat until he forgot himself in the sweet oblivion of her body?

"A love match," he said, using her words. "That was what you wished to have had yourself."

"Yes," she said softly.

He could have kicked himself in the arse anew at the hesitation in her voice. "It is my turn to offer my contrition. It was not my intention to dredge up painful memories or make a mockery of your engagement with our...understanding."

"I believe I may have misjudged you. Initially, when you announced that we were betrothed, I supposed you were in need of my dowry, which Father continues to raise in hopes he can see me settled."

There was a note of irritation in her voice now. He found himself wanting to chase it. But there was guilt, too. Because he did require a dowry to save his estates from ruin. But that wasn't why he'd feigned their betrothal. Nor was it why he'd spent the most glorious moments of his life yesterday beneath her petticoats.

"You said you believe yourself incapable of happiness."

And what a travesty that would be. A bold, beautiful, vibrant woman like Lady Clementine Hammond never finding her own contentedness after doing her utmost to make so many other couples realize theirs.

"I do."

Before she could say more, a flurry of footsteps in the

gravel broke the silence, along with a low, husky laugh and the undeniable sound of kissing. *Good heavens.* Not only were they not alone in the gardens, but their fellow guests were up to mischief.

Mischief?

Christ. Since when had he become the spinster duenna of this entire affair? He would have been disgusted were he not so cognizant of the fact that if they did not wish to chance being caught alone together *again*, they had to move.

"Come," he whispered, offering her his arm. "We've got to make our way out of here before we are seen."

She took it and clung to him as the footsteps came nearer.

Another low round of female chuckles and a masculine growl split the night.

CHAPTER 9

"Locked," Dorset announced grimly.

They had spent an indeterminate span of time wandering through the moonlit gardens in an effort to avoid being caught alone together. For part of the time, she had been convinced they were lost. The marquess, however, had been adamant they were not.

"Are you certain this is the east wing?" she asked him, biting her lip to keep from saying more.

She was reasonably certain they were at the west wing of the manor house.

"This is the conservatory," he insisted. "These doors were open just the other night."

"It looks more like the library to me," she could not help but to counter. "The conservatory is all windows, and not nearly so much stone."

"I am utterly certain this is the conservatory."

She pursed her lips. "You were also certain we were not heading into the maze earlier, and yet we were."

He sighed. "Need you remind me?"

"I was merely pointing out that you are not a perfect navigator."

He cast a glance over his shoulder as he toyed with the door handles. Although his face was primarily shadowed, she swore his gaze burned her through the darkness. "I am an *excellent* navigator."

"If you were excellent at navigating, we would not have spent the last hour wandering through the Duchess of Bradford's gardens. And now, we're quite trapped outside the house, alone in the dark, our reputations at stake."

"You are being unnecessarily dramatic, my dear. We will find our way into the house one way or another."

"I hardly think I am being dramatic, unnecessarily or otherwise," she said, gathering steam. "Indeed, I—"

But her words were smothered in the next moment.

By the Marquess of Dorset's lips.

And sweet heaven above, his lips were ambrosia. Sliding her arms around his neck and kissing him back seemed like the only sensible option. The night cloaked them in velvety darkness. His masculine scent teased her senses. He was so strong and warm. He tasted of sweet wine with a hint of the bite of tobacco. Strangely, she did not mind it on him.

His tongue dipped into her mouth, and she opened. Oh, this was wicked. He kissed marvelously well, kissed her with a familiarity that stole her breath, knowing just what she wanted. What she needed. And as before, his kisses lit fires within her.

Raging, furious fires.

She pressed herself shamelessly into him, her breasts crushing against his chest. Her nipples were hard and aching. A fluttering sensation had begun in her belly and traveled lower, settling between her thighs as surely as if his mouth were there, pleasuring her as he'd done before. Driving her to the edge of reason, to the dizzying heights of sensual madness.

He pulled his mouth from hers, but the kiss was not over yet. Instead, he dragged his lips along her jaw, as if he were savoring her, as if he couldn't bear to remove his lips from her body. When he kissed her throat, a new bolt of desire slid through her. This kiss was every bit as incendiary. Her head fell back. He sucked on her skin. Hot, openmouthed kisses trailed to her collarbone. His hands were on her waist, gripping her and holding her steady when her knees threatened to give way.

She tunneled her fingers through his hair. It was surprisingly soft and silken.

His knowing lips traveled to the place where her throat met her shoulder. The cut of her décolletage left her flesh bare for his exploration. There, he nibbled lightly. A sigh escaped her. She was hopelessly caught in the sensual spell he wove around her.

Belatedly, she recalled he had silenced her with a kiss. How high-handed of him. She ought to have delivered a blistering setdown. Instead, her determination had melted just the same as the rest of her. She needed to recall all the reasons why she should never fall beneath the spell of a rake again.

For this was what rakehells did, was it not? They kissed ladies senseless in darkened alcoves and moonlit gardens. They slipped into bedchamber windows and whispered false promises and lured innocent misses into sin. They kissed too well, knew how to bring women untold pleasures.

Except, Walter's kisses were but a pale, tepid memory now, and the marquess's hand was mired in her skirts, lifting her hems. They slid sinuously over her calves, above her knees, cool night air licking at her skin. And she wanted more. She wanted to lie in the grass and pull Dorset atop her, to feel his delicious weight and masculine strength, wanted for him to put his mouth where he had before. Her sex ached and pulsed at the prospect, and then his knowing caress was glanced over her drawers.

Thank heavens she was wearing them this evening. Sanity returned to her.

She jerked away from Dorset, her heart pounding, breath ragged. He allowed her to go without any protest. How she wished she could see his countenance. But the shadows and the night obscured much of his face.

"We will never find ourselves back inside if we continue in such a manner," she told him, despising herself for the throaty hoarseness of her voice, the evidence of just how badly he'd affected her.

He scrubbed a hand over his jaw. "It seemed an excellent way to keep you from chastising me."

"I was not chastising you," she argued, needing something to say, some reason why she shouldn't throw herself back into the marquess's arms and beg him for more.

"Hmm," was all he said.

The longer they lingered in the darkness together, away from the rest of the house party, the greater their chances of discovery. There also remained the possibility they would be seen should they travel back down the path from which they had come. They were not alone in the gardens, and the couple who had chanced into the moonlight for an assignation likely remained somewhere out there.

Desperate, she swept past the marquess, seizing the door herself.

"Locked," she grumbled.

"As I said." His voice was at her shoulder. Wry and far too near. "Did you think I was lying merely so that I could seduce you out here in the wet grass? Darling, let me reassure you, if I want to seduce you, I'll choose a far more amenable location to do so."

More awareness prickled through her. Why did he have to be so skilled at kissing? So vexingly smug about his sensual prowess? Why did he have to make her knees go weak and her body restless with wanting?

Her thumb traveled over the lock. Life with an elder sister who had adored playing cruel tricks on her by locking her in rooms had imbued Clementine with the ability to free herself. When one was desperate, one also became quite creative.

She reached into her carefully styled coiffure, feeling about for hairpins. Finding one, she pulled it free and then jammed the end into the lock.

"What are you doing?" Dorset asked.

This time, he stood in such proximity that she swore she could feel the warmth of his breath upon her neck.

She sent him a nettled glare. "Attempting to get us into the library."

"I am certain it is the conservatory, as I said." There was a pause, then, "You are trying to pick the lock?"

"No, I am building a boat," she said. "Of course I am trying to pick the lock. Have you any other suggestions?"

"Would more kissing be out of the question?"

No.

"Yes," she snapped, working the hairpin deeper into the lock's inner mechanism. "You truly are a despicable rake."

"A rake, perhaps. But you did not seem to think me so despicable a few moments ago when your tongue was in my mouth."

Her hairpin dropped to the ground from suddenly numb fingers, landing on the gravel path with a distinct *ping*.

"Lord Dorset," she sputtered, sure she should be outraged

he would dare to refer to her response to his passionate kisses so directly.

"Ambrose," he reminded her, his tone silky.

She had to cling to her defenses. To formality. The Marquess of Dorset was dangerous. In an attempt to distract herself, she sank low to the ground, trying to locate her hairpin.

"You shan't find it in the darkness," he said.

But then he had sunk to his haunches as well, and his fingers were traversing the moss-and-gravel path far too close to hers. Their fingers brushed. Once. Twice.

The third time sent a new wave of desire washing over her.

She paused. "I suppose I shall have to use another. My lady's maid is a deft hand at using as few pins as possible. I hesitate to remove one more lest the whole effort come tumbling down."

"Here it is." His tone was triumphant, his eyes glinting in the moonlight along with the flash of his even, pearly teeth as he grinned.

She plucked the pin from his fingers. "That was an extraordinary burst of luck. Perhaps fate's fickle wheel is deciding to give us a good turn after all."

"Blame it on fate all you like, but I have extremely skilled fingers."

Clementine could not stop the hitch in her breath at his sinful words as she rose and turned back to her efforts at the lock, remembering indeed just how skillful the Marquess of Dorset's fingers had proven. Nor could she quell the yearning spreading through her.

She wanted him to kiss her again, heaven help her. But no, she must not allow it. To do so would be wrong. Just as wrong as allowing this feigned betrothal of theirs to continue would be.

I despise rakes, she reminded herself firmly.

But then his hand settled on her waist with the familiarity of a lover, and her hand jolted, longing pooling between her thighs.

"Damn and blast," she hissed.

"A shocking curse from such lovely lips," he said behind her, his tone provoking, his fingers on her waist giving a gentle squeeze. "Never say you have dropped the hairpin again."

Dear heavens, she liked his hands on her. Liked his touch far, far too much.

"I have not." With renewed persistence, she jammed the hairpin into the mechanism. But it was proving stubbornly insistent. There was no hope for it. She was going to have to use a second hairpin to make a lever.

Praying her hair did not come unraveling around her shoulders, she felt about for a second pin and removed it. Fortunately, her hair still seemed relatively stable, so she returned to the art of picking the lock. After bending the second pin to the angle she required, she slid it inside, then used the other pin to press about for a vulnerability.

"Will you be needing a third hairpin?"

Dorset's voice, so near to her left ear yet again, gave her a start. She cried out, the sound echoing in the gardens, reverberating off the gravel and hedges and the stone of the main house wall.

"Did I startle you?" His voice was amused now. "Forgive me. But you really must try to keep quiet. What if someone should overhear you and come looking for us before you're able to pick the lock?"

Clementine refused to respond. She turned the hairpin, pressed forward, and found the right spot. The lock opened.

"Thank heavens," she said on a sigh of relief. "You see, Dorset? This *is*, in fact, the library, just as I told you."

But her relief and jubilation were short-lived. For as the library door swung open and they crossed the threshold together, they discovered that the dimly lit room with its two-tiered walls of books wasn't empty.

Lady Edith was within—there was no mistaking that vibrant copper hair. Her mere presence was hardly shocking. However, she wasn't alone. And she was wrapped in the arms of a tall, dark-haired man.

~

"Well, hell," Ambrose muttered at the sight before him as, at his side, Lady Clementine simultaneously gasped.

Valentine Blakemoor, the notorious self-made property magnate and one of the wealthiest men in England, raised his head and pinned them both with an unrelenting stare.

"We've visitors, it would seem," he drawled to the lady in his arms, not bothering to step away from her or engage in any pretense that he hadn't just been kissing her senseless.

He simply gazed at Ambrose and Clementine coolly, impassively, as if he'd been caught in the act of nothing more ordinary than escorting a lady through a country reel in a ballroom. His partner, however, did not appear nearly as unmoved by their interruption.

Lady Edith Smythe blinked owlishly at them from behind her spectacles, still wrapped in Blakemoor's embrace.

"Lady Clementine," she said weakly, her cheeks flaming to rival the brilliant color of her hair. "Lord Dorset."

Belatedly, she wriggled free of Blakemoor's hold. The man's arms fell away, and he took a step back, his countenance still utterly devoid of expression. Ambrose didn't know Blakemoor well, although they ran in some of the same circles. They'd crossed paths for the first time in months upon their arrival at the house party. But the man's reputation preceded him. It was said that Blakemoor had risen from the gutters with dogged persistence, ruthlessly working until he'd amassed an astonishing amount of wealth. His presence at the Duchess of Bradford's house party was a testament to just how far he'd come.

"We were taking the air," Clementine announced brightly, "and we became turned around in the maze. We thought to simply let ourselves into the library and find our way back to the evening's entertainments."

The entertainments being Miss Hortense Sinclair's dreadful caterwauling. Ambrose winced. One could only hope she had finished her efforts by now.

"It would seem that we had almost the same thought," Lady Edith said, flashing what appeared to be a false smile. "Mr. Blakemoor was kind enough to escort me to the library in search of a volume I've been looking for."

Ambrose highly doubted that Blakemoor had been looking for anything more than Lady Edith's lips, but he wisely refrained from saying so. He reckoned the gentlemanly thing to do was to pretend they hadn't caught Lady Edith and Blakemoor in a passionate embrace.

"Perhaps we can all return to the music room together," he suggested pleasantly. "Before our absences are noted."

He could only imagine the horror Lady Edith's mother would endure should she realize her precious daughter had been caught in the clutches of a baseborn businessman instead of being politely escorted about by a duke as she no doubt hoped.

Blakemoor raised a brow, looking singularly disinterested. "I fear I'm too tired for more musical diversion this evening. I believe I'll retire to my room. Dorset, I trust you'll see Lady Edith back to the safety of her mother's loving protection."

"Of course," he promised easily, noting the barbed undercurrent in the other man's words.

He found himself wondering just what was afoot between Blakemoor and the quiet, unassuming Lady Edith. Ambrose wouldn't have wagered the freckled wallflower would draw the attention of a sybarite such as the rakish businessman. Blakemoor's proclivity for debauchery was well-known, and Lady Edith, in comparison, rather resembled nothing so much as a mouse in the presence of a lion.

"My lady." With a mocking bow in Lady Edith's direction, Blakemoor took his leave, prowling from the library.

Lady Edith watched him go, looking rather forlorn.

"Well then," Clementine said with forced cheer. "We shall get you back to your dragon mama's side before she begins breathing fire, my dear Lady Edith. Shan't we, Dorset?"

He cleared his throat, trying not to notice how beautiful Clementine looked, her mouth thoroughly kissed. Trying not to want her more than he wanted his next breath.

And failing miserably.

"So we shall," he said, offering the ladies each an arm.

As he swept them both from the room, a very alarming realization occurred to him.

He was becoming besotted with Lady Clementine Hammond. It was as if she possessed some manner of hold upon him, manacles of steel which his will had yet to break. There it was, plain as the nose on his face. A stark, unexpected, and decidedly unpleasant truth. Tonight's revelations had gone a long way toward explaining her incessant matchmaking schemes.

Now, he understood she had a heart.

And somehow, that knowledge had made his own heart—frigid since Anna's defection—soften. The inconvenient lust he had experienced for Clementine from the moment of his arrival had deepened and…

Changed.

Mayhap *he* had changed.

Had he? God. This would never do. Perhaps the only answer to his dilemma was to end their feigned betrothal sooner rather than later and to leave the house party with as much haste as possible.

CHAPTER 10

The hour was late, but Clementine couldn't sleep.

She was pacing the Axminster in her guest chamber, bare feet padding along the thick, woolen carpets, caught in the grip of an exceedingly large, Marquess-of-Dorset-shaped problem.

She couldn't stop thinking about him. Couldn't stop longing for him. Her body remained alive with the promise he had awakened in her, and she had no answer for it. No amount of trying to read, of tossing and turning in her bed, or attempting to give herself some much-needed relief had helped. Her own touch was a pale comparison to Dorset's sinful mouth. She had brought herself to crescendo by pressing her fingers to her aching flesh, but it hadn't been enough.

Frustrated, she'd fled the bed and resorted to pacing. But not even that expenditure of energy would do.

She was aching for one man alone.

Aching for completion.

It was wrong, and it was most unwise. It was a flagrant

disavowal of her every promise to herself in the wake of Walter's betrayal. And yet, she couldn't seem to help herself.

She wanted the Marquess of Dorset.

Ambrose.

Her betrothed.

Her heart beat faster, and she banished the thought instantly. For he wasn't her betrothed, and that was the problem. He was a careless rake, a devotee of pleasure, an inconstant seducer. He might have believed he loved Lady Anna Harcastle, but everyone knew he'd needed her dowry.

A sudden sound interrupted her turbulent ruminations. Surely it wasn't a knock. She paused, not even realizing she was holding her breath until she heard it again, a tap at her door so faint it might not have been there at all.

Without hesitation, she hastened to the latch, opening the door to peer into the hall to find an all too familiar form looming in the shadows. One she'd recognize anywhere.

"Dorset," she whispered, shocked that he would take such a tremendous risk and then realizing anyone might venture into the hall and see him standing there at half past one, at her bedroom door. "Come in," she added, stepping aside to allow him entrance.

He obeyed her command, crossing the threshold silently, his emerald gaze shining brilliantly in the low gaslight she'd kept lit. She closed the door, and the two of them were alone. The air between them was suddenly electric, heavy with pent-up possibility. He was dressed in shirtsleeves and a waistcoat and tweed trousers, his necktie and coat notably absent. His dark hair was ruffled, as if he'd been passing his long fingers through it.

She thought then that he was the most beautiful sight she'd ever beheld. Painfully handsome. Everything she wanted and yet should not have. He was wrong for her, bad for her, dangerous to her virtue and her heart.

"What are you doing here?" she demanded, irritated with herself for her unwanted reaction.

For the longing that had kept her from sleep.

"I think it would be best if I leave the house party early," he said.

Which was not at all what she had expected to hear. Disappointment, sharp and shocking, cut through her.

"You've come to my chamber in the midst of the night to tell me that?" she asked, moving to put some distance between them as she ventured toward the low fire that had been laid by a servant on account of the damp, chill evening.

He nodded, his gaze traveling over her body as if it were a caress. "You were awake."

It would do no good to lie; he could plainly see by the blazing gas lamp and her haste in opening the door that she'd neither been asleep nor abed.

"I was," she admitted warily, wondering what he was after. "You've taken a great risk in coming here. If anyone saw you—"

"No one saw me," he interrupted, moving toward her. "I made sure of it."

"If you're discovered in my chamber, no amount of explaining will persuade anyone that you haven't taken liberties with me," she reminded him sharply, clinging to her sense of reason.

This was foolish. He was plying his rakish wiles, and she wouldn't fall into his trap.

"I'm aware," he said, stopping near enough for her to touch, his gaze flitting over her again. "You aren't wearing a dressing gown, darling."

She glanced down at herself, belatedly realizing she was clad in nothing more than her night rail and that it was likely so thin that it was transparent. The peaks of her breasts poked beneath the fabric, stiff and jutting wantonly toward him as if in offering.

Clementine decided to brazen it out, lifting her chin. "I'm in the privacy of my chamber. Why should I?"

"Because I can't think with you standing there in that wisp of a gown," he rasped. "I can see your damned nipples."

Heat pooled low in her belly at his wicked words. She crossed her arms over her breasts to shield them from him, telling herself she would remain impervious to his charm.

"Pray say what you've come to and then be gone," she told him coolly.

"I wanted to warn you about my departure," he elaborated, his voice dripping over her like warm honey. "If I leave in haste, it will create a scandal, and I've no wish to cause you further trouble or to ruin my future chances of securing a bride. We'll need to work out a plan to politely break off our engagement. Perhaps a small scene tomorrow in which you voice your displeasure with something I've done."

She couldn't quell the new dismay rising inside her like a tide at his words. His future chances of securing a bride? He wished to marry someone else? Why did she find the notion so terrible? He wasn't here intent upon seduction, then. Rather, he had come to her so that they could formulate a means of his escape.

"Is our feigned betrothal so repugnant to you then, that you can't bear to endure it for the duration of the fortnight?" she asked crisply, hating herself for the edge of hurt that laced her voice against her will.

Why should she be hurt? She didn't even like the man. She certainly had no wish to marry him. The sooner they ended this charade, the better. The sooner he never touched or kissed her again, the better.

"Is that what you think?" he returned, instead of answering her question.

"What else am I meant to think? You barged into my room in the midst of the night to tell me you're leaving tomorrow."

He had come nearer to her, and somehow in her pique, she'd failed to take note. But now he was hovering over her, tall and insufferably handsome.

Tempting, too.

"First," he said softly, "I didn't barge in here. I knocked."

She raised a brow. "You're being deliberately obtuse, and I don't like it. Just make up whatever excuse you wish tomorrow and be gone."

"Damn it, Clementine, I'm trying to do the right thing by you." He raked a hand through his hair.

Even in his exasperation, she wanted him. Wanted to seal her lips over his and kiss him. Wanted to be in his arms. In his bed.

"You should have done the right thing that day in the gardens instead of inventing this preposterous betrothal," she snapped, quite miffed with herself for her inability to banish the inconvenient yearning.

She had been so very careful after Walter. And somehow, this beautiful rakehell of a marquess had toppled her every wall of defense, leaving her helpless.

"I tried."

"Did you? One must wonder." She moved to stalk past him, but he stayed her with a hand on her arm.

Such searing heat went through her that it was a miracle she wasn't burned.

"Of course I did. Do you doubt it? Surely you understand that is also the reason I must go."

"So that you may leave and carry on with your search for a suitable bride," she said, trying to wrest her arm free of his grasp, hating herself for the effect he had on her. For the petulance in her voice. For somehow being hurt by his abrupt defection when it was nothing less than what she should have come to expect from a rake, to say nothing of what she should have wanted.

Had she learned nothing from Walter?

It would seem not.

"That's not the reason," he said quietly.

She stiffened, wishing he would release her, wishing she were wearing something more substantial than her night rail, for she may as well have been naked before him. "What is, then?"

"The reason is this." He pulled her against him, taking her by such surprise that she fell into the delicious hardness of his chest, and before she could catch her wits, his mouth was on hers.

Kissing.

Claiming.

And although heaven knew she should be pushing him away, she didn't want to. She wanted him closer. His decadent scent curled around her, and she wrapped her arms about his neck, pressing herself against him, glorying in the hard ridge of him pressed into her belly. He desired her.

Everything about the way he held her, the way he kissed her, his body's reaction to her, told her so. She gloried in that knowledge, opening for his questing tongue and meeting him with a tentative parry of her own. He groaned into the kiss, and she sank her fingers into the rich, soft strands of his hair, cradling his head as she answered his lips with hers.

One of his hands was splayed over her lower back, and the other cupped her cheek with a reverence that astonished her. He pressed her even closer, consuming her with his mouth, his tongue sliding sinuously against hers. He tasted like wine and sin and everything she'd been missing these last few lonely years of self-imposed isolation from the male sex. And she couldn't help but wonder why she had forced herself to keep away when she had been missing this glorious thrill, this perilous bliss.

Her heart was no longer vulnerable to conscienceless rakes. But her body was not nearly so inured to seduction. And now that Dorset was here in her chamber, their bodies perfectly aligned, his lips devouring hers, she didn't care about consequences or the danger to her reputation or anything else. All she cared about was him.

Of having more of him.

The hand on the small of her back dipped, sliding over her rump to capture it, giving her a firm squeeze and grinding her against his rigidness as he did so. She moaned, sucking on his tongue, thinking of how it had felt to have his fingers inside her. Wondering what it would feel like to have this part of him inside her instead. For she was not unaware of what transpired between a man and a woman—at least, not the general mechanics of sexual congress.

Her knees went weak and she clung to him, and then his hand moved again, and he was pressing against that most sensitive place, from behind, his wicked fingers sinking into her willing flesh, making her want him more. Another silly, feminine noise of surrender slipped from her, and she would have been ashamed of herself were she not so swept away in the overflowing river of desire.

He tore his lips from hers, looking down at her with a hooded stare and eyes that smoldered with sensual intent. "This is why I have to go, Clementine. I don't trust myself with you. You're the most vexing woman I've ever met. You confound me and infuriate me, and you tore my future asunder with your bloody meddling, and there's no earthly reason why I should want you the way I do." The hand on her backside flexed, his fingers finding the place where she wanted him most.

His words stunned her. They were terribly unflattering—

at least, most of them. And she was equally mystified by her reaction to him. Because not even his grim pronouncement could soothe the ache of yearning deep inside her.

"I hate rakes," she told him, all too aware that, despite her best intentions, she didn't hate him.

Not at all.

They stared at each other, both breathless, their mouths dark from drugging kisses, their bodies entwined, desire so thick it could have been cut with a knife.

"This is wrong," he murmured. "I need to marry."

"And I have no intention of marrying," she hastened to say, heart pounding, body desperate with need.

"I should leave."

"Sherborne Manor?" She clung to him more tightly, as if to keep him with her. "Now? It's the midst of the night."

He chuckled softly. "Your chamber, darling. I should leave your chamber. If I don't…"

"If you don't?" she prompted, holding her breath.

For a moment, she feared he wouldn't answer. That he would simply untangle himself from her embrace and retreat altogether, leaving her here, unfulfilled and aching for him. But then he rubbed his thumb over her cheekbone with agonizing slowness, as if he committed the structure of her face to his memory with the act.

"I won't stop until you're naked under me in that bed and I'm inside you," he said, voice low and rough.

And it was precisely what she'd longed to hear for all the wrong reasons. But she couldn't seem to stop herself.

"Then don't stop," she told him.

"Clementine." His tone was laden with meaning. A warning, perhaps.

One she ignored. In for a penny, et cetera.

"Ambrose," she countered, using his given name. "Don't stop."

"Bloody hell," he growled, crushing her lips beneath his.

It was as if all the restraint he possessed had come suddenly crashing down, and she reveled in his loss of control. For the past few years, she had lived a life above reproach. She had thrown herself into the sometimes thankless task of arranging happiness for others whilst ignoring her own, casting it aside and pretending as if her own secret yearnings could forever be banished. But her reaction to him was proof—incontrovertible—that she couldn't suppress this part of herself. She was still the same wicked, wanton creature who had succumbed to Walter's persuasive kisses. Only, she was wiser now. She knew what to expect. Disappointment could only sting the first time.

And she forgot about disappointment entirely then, because Ambrose was moving them. Kissing her senseless and guiding them toward her bed. They stopped at the edge of the mattress, and she grew impatient with all the layers keeping him from her. She found the buttons of his waistcoat, cool and metallic, and slipped them from their moorings with ease.

He shrugged it away without moving his lips from hers. Her fingers were unsteady by the time she reached for the closures on his shirt, and he replaced hers easily with his, tearing at the entire affair until the sound of buttons raining on the floor pierced her erotic delirium.

She broke the kiss, staring up at him. "You've ruined your shirt."

"I've ruined far more important things in my life," he said, and then he kissed her again and she forgot to fret over lost buttons on her bedroom floor.

Forgot everything but him when he tossed his shirt away and her hands were blessedly free to roam his bare, heated skin, glorying in the hardness and strength lying just beneath the surface. He was all muscle and sinew and bone, his chest dotted with a smattering of crisp hairs, his shoulders broad and strong, his abdomen lean, and when she ran her hand down a trail that led to the waistband of his trousers, his muscles went taut.

"Clementine," he murmured against her lips. "You surprise me, darling."

She hoped he meant that in a good way. She couldn't be sure. But it didn't matter when he took her traveling hand in his and guided it lower, to where his cock rose ready and thick beneath his country tweed.

"This is what you do to me, darling," he told her, his mouth a scant inch from hers, his hot breath coasting over her lips.

How impossibly large and intimidating he felt beneath her untutored hand. Her fingers sought the shape of him, long and thick, and he groaned, pressing his forehead to hers, kissing her swiftly before raising his head again.

"Now is when you should tell me to go," he said hoarsely, his hips thrusting him deeper into her hand.

"Do you want to go?" she asked boldly, feeling suddenly powerful at the effect she had on him.

More powerful than she'd ever felt before.

"God no," he confessed with a half chuckle.

"Then stay." She stroked him through his trousers, learning how he felt, what he liked, wanting to bring him pleasure as he had done for her that day in the library.

"Open my trousers," he told her. "Touch me."

Permission.

Almost giddy, she did as he asked, trembling fingers flying over fastenings until the placket opened, and he sprang forth, even larger than she had supposed, filling her hand. She wrapped her fingers around him, wondering how he would fit inside her and yet needing it so badly, a hollow ache inside her pulsing and demanding, making her helpless to do anything but follow her desire.

"Yes," he hissed, looking down to where she gripped his erect length, as if the sight mesmerized him.

She followed his gaze, looking her fill and finding it equally erotic, her pale hand on his demanding, ruddy cock. As she watched, he grew harder, longer, and an answering pang of need trilled deep within her. He was surprisingly smooth and soft here, vulnerable in a way the rest of his body was not, and yet still so thoroughly masculine, so potent and powerful.

"Stroke me," he ordered her softly.

She did, tentatively moving her grasp up and down his shaft, from base to tip, until he'd let out another groan and a bead of moisture had seeped from the slit on the blunt head of his cock. Something came over her then, some overwhelming need that would later shock her when she thought of it, but she didn't care now. She wanted to taste him as he had tasted her. Clementine rubbed her thumb over the pearlescent drop, and then she brought it to her lips, her tongue darting out for a taste.

A growl started deep in his throat, and then he was tearing at his trousers, tearing at her nightgown, and in a blinding rush of frenzied need, they were both naked on her bed. Ambrose was atop her, Clementine's legs parted to accommodate him, and he lowered his head to her breasts, sucking one hungry nipple into his mouth.

The pull of his sinful mouth on her sent liquid heat to pool between her thighs, where she could already feel she'd become quite wet. It was a singular sensation, one she'd known before when he'd kissed her in his chamber and when he'd seduced her in the library. She shouldn't like it at all, but to her great shame, she very much did.

All thoughts of propriety, of avoiding scandal, of the

reasons why she shouldn't be giving herself to a rake vanished. She threaded her fingers through his hair with one hand, watching the dusky strands fall as if seeing everything for the first time. And deep in her heart, in a place she'd thought long locked away, the reason for her lack of control burned like a brand.

She was falling in love with this scoundrel.

Mere days was all it had required. It was impossible, improbable, and yet...true.

Later, when her mind was not so filled with fire, she would consider this most unwanted discovery and ponder what she was to do about it. Now, his tongue was flicking over her nipple with wicked intent, and she ran her hand down the broad plane of his back in approval. He lapped at her, licked her, sucked. And then he moved to her other breast, his hot mouth gliding over her everywhere she wanted him, his teeth gently nipping. He leveraged himself on one arm and his other hand was busy caressing over her stomach, his palm flattening there for a moment as he pressed, intensifying the ache between her legs.

But then his hand shifted, and his fingers slicked over her folds, using her own wetness against her. He worked over the bud of her sex that was so gloriously sensitive, still suckling the peak of her breast, and she jolted beneath him, pleasure soaring through her. Her heart was pounding, and she was awash with sensation. Everything was new, even herself. She was incredibly attuned to his body, so powerful and strong, the weight of him pressing her into the soft mattress, to the rake of his stubble over her bare breast, the flicker of his tongue, the slow, maddening pressure over her sex.

Her hips danced beneath him, seeking more, searching for that wondrous height he'd taken her to before. The pull of his mouth on her breast was too much. He pressed harder, faster, working her nub as she did in the privacy of darkness, alone in her bed. But it was better, because it was his touch. Because it was him.

Ambrose.

He released her nipple and slanted a languid, mossy gaze up at her. "Yes, darling?"

She realized she must have moaned his name aloud in her frenzy. "More," she gasped as he continued plying her sex with the same wicked torture, rolling his thumb over her now, stimulating her to the edge of reason before retreating again with light, slow strokes that drove her mad. "I need more."

"You do, don't you?" He smiled wickedly and kissed the hollow between her breasts, inhaling deeply. "You're so deliciously wet."

His words made an embarrassing rush of moisture pool there, where he was touching her. But he didn't seem to mind. Instead, he made a deep noise of approval and stroked her some more, trailing a finger along her seam until he hovered just above her entrance. One push, and he'd be inside her, and she wanted that more than anything.

"Please," she begged breathlessly, licking her lips, body undulating in search of his. "Don't torment me so."

"Patience. I want to give you pleasure before I take you." He kissed the curve of her breast. Kissed lower.

Oh dear heavens, surely he wasn't thinking of doing *that* again, was he?

"You have," she protested, breath coming in harder pants now, pulse swiftly picking up its pace in anticipation.

His mouth kept going, bestowing a string of hot kisses past her navel, pausing for his tongue to dip into the shallow little hollow and send an exquisite frisson of pleasure coursing through her.

He lifted his head to give her a rogue's smile. "But not enough."

His hands moved to her inner thighs, soothing, caressing, pushing them farther apart to make room.

"You needn't," she protested with a politeness she would have thought beyond her.

"Oh, but I do," he said darkly, and then his mouth descended, and his tongue was on her, and she thought she might explode from the wondrousness of it.

She curled her toes into the bedclothes and grasped handfuls of sheets in both hands, surrendering herself to his lips and tongue. And oh heavens, to his fingers. Because it wasn't enough for him to tease her with long and steady licks to her pearl, and he sank a finger inside her deep, so deep. She tensed around him instantly, the penetration enough to carry her over the edge.

Still, her climax took her by surprise, roaring through her as she threw back her head into the pillow and cried out without a thought for the ramifications of being overheard. He stayed with her as she shattered and returned to herself, his mouth as greedy as it had been when he'd been kissing her lips.

He only raised his head for a moment, his lips glistening with her wetness, to warn, "Quieter, darling."

And then his face was buried between her thighs again, and he was licking and sucking, a second finger joining the first, stretching her, filling her. He was moving in and out in strokes that deepened, his fingers finding a place that made black stars waltz around the edges of her vision. It was intense, impossible. Surely he didn't expect her to reach her pinnacle again?

"One more time," he crooned, his fingers surging in and out, before he sucked hard on her tender bud.

He did.

"I couldn't possibly," she gasped.

"Oh, you could." He licked. "You can." Kissed. "You will." *Bit.*

And he made a liar of her, for she did, the second spasm seizing her as his teeth tugged on her swollen pearl and his fingers curled, finding a place of unbelievable bliss. She came and pressed a hand over her mouth to stifle her cry as a flood of wetness poured from her, bathing his hand, his face.

She was awash in the glow of her release and yet acutely aware of how soaked she was, how messy. A slight tinge of embarrassment cut sharply through her ecstasy. "Forgive me," she gasped.

But far from being repelled, he had withdrawn his fingers and was licking her up as if she were the world's greatest feast.

"So good, my darling," he praised, lapping at her before pressing a wet kiss to her inner thigh.

He shifted again, positioning himself so that he was between her spread legs, and she was no longer ashamed of her body's reaction to his. Everything about this felt right, even as she knew how wrong it was. He covered her, the crisp hairs of his chest abrading her nipples, his heat surrounding her. Everything she saw was Ambrose, his painfully handsome face, the shadow of stubble shading his sharp jaw, the fullness of his lips, the angular delineation of his clavicle as he leveraged himself over her, the dark hair falling rakishly over his brow.

He smoothed his lips over her temple, kissed her ear. "How gentle should I be, darling?"

Her arms went around him of their own accord, and she was clinging to him like a vine. The searing deliciousness of his body pressed to hers was enough to rob her of the ability to think for a moment. And she had to take a deep breath, chase the fog of desire from her mind, and realize what he was truly asking.

"I don't know," she answered honestly, breathlessly.

He tensed, raising his head to stare down at her. "You're a virgin?"

Had he thought she wasn't? She didn't think she'd given him cause to believe otherwise, but then, she had alluded to having been betrayed by a rake. Certainly, her lack of decorum with Ambrose himself would have called her past experience into question. But Walter, for all his many faults, had left that part of her untouched, if not her heart.

"Yes," she murmured, suddenly nervous, afraid that it would change things.

That he would retreat.

But he didn't. Instead, he trailed kisses along her jaw. "Gentle, then."

She wasn't sure she wanted gentle, but nothing mattered in the next moment, because his mouth found hers, and he kissed her slowly, sweetly, deeply. And it didn't feel like the kiss of a stranger, a man whose courtship of her had been feigned. Rather, it felt like the kiss of a man who wanted her, who cherished her, who desired her desperately enough to take her and yet put her pleasure before his own.

Clementine lost track of everything that wasn't Ambrose then. The outside world ceased to exist. Everything beyond the walls of her guest chamber vanished, and there was only his body on hers, the teasing of his fingers over her throbbing sex, his lips on hers. She was writhing beneath him, ready, impossibly, for more, when he replaced his fingers with his rigid cock, gliding the blunt tip through her folds and making her bow toward him in welcome. In need.

Wordlessly, he gave her what she wanted. Suddenly, he was there, where she was aching, just where she needed him. There was pressure, so much, his body sliding against hers, and then into hers, as if she had been fashioned for him and this was where he had always been meant to be. His thickness was lodged inside her, stretching her, making her ache in a new way, and it wasn't at all what she had expected. Rather, it was so much more. She felt the urge to move, but he paused, breaking the kiss, to look down at her.

"Gentle enough?" he asked, his voice strained.

She shifted restlessly, feeling strangely frustrated. "Too gentle, perhaps."

"My beautiful, wicked girl," he breathed, and then he hooked her legs around his waist and he thrust hard and deep, until he was all the way inside her and they were hip to hip, chest to chest.

One.

She gasped at the new feeling of it, of him, throbbing and sheathed to the hilt and big. So very big. It was exquisite, pleasure on the border of pain, and she never wanted him to leave her. She wanted to keep him like this forever.

"I'm going to move now," he told her.

Clementine was vaguely sure she knew what that meant, but he swiftly proved her wrong, because he withdrew almost entirely and then pushed inside her again, his movement aided by her wetness, gliding with an ease that surprised her. And then he did it again, suckling her breast as he pumped in and out of her, and the new feelings changed again. Something inside her tightened almost unbearably. He sucked hard on her breast, thrusting, groaning against her, his eyes closed as he lost himself to the feelings.

She didn't dare close her eyes because she didn't want to miss a single moment. She watched the beautiful, fluid motions of his body moving with a grace that belied the carnal, raw act he performed, alternating between her breasts, suckling her until she couldn't stand it a second more, and she shattered, another cry torn from her lips as she rode out yet another blissful peak. She tightened on him, and he groaned, pumping into her faster, harder, until he released her nipple and buried his face in her throat, slipping free of her as he groaned his own release.

She felt the hot, wet spurt of his seed on her inner thigh and stomach, felt the stickiness of it as his full weight came atop her. Felt his heart pounding against her chest, the silken softness of his hair rasping against her cheek. And she wrapped her arms around his neck and held him close to her, knowing she would never be the same.

CHAPTER 11

"Winston," Ambrose said contemplatively to his valet that morning as the redoubtable man was in the midst of shaving him, careful not to move his jaw too much, "I believe I'm in need of some sound advice."

He was going to marry Lady Clementine Hammond.

Rather, he was going to have to *persuade* her to marry him. A task that seemed far more daunting by the morning light than it had been in the night, when her body had been soft and delicious and pliant beneath his. He'd been buried deep inside her when he'd reached the inevitable conclusion that she was his, that he had to have her as his wife, that this all-consuming passion for her was unlike any he'd ever felt for another, unlike any he'd ever feel again, and that it wouldn't fade. That having her had not slaked his hunger, but only made him want her more.

For the first time, he'd felt utterly at peace. For a hardened, seasoned rake such as himself, it had been damned disarming, to say the least. And yet, he had to marry her, and not just because he had made love to her. Twice.

No, he had to marry her because it was the practical thing

to do. He wanted her. She wanted him. They were already betrothed. He required a dowry; she had an excellent one. They suited in bed, if nowhere else. And then he could further explore the delights of her beautiful body. Not a hardship, that.

"I'm happy to be of service, sir," Winston said calmly, dragging the razor over a patch of skin on Ambrose's chin. "What manner of advice?"

Ambrose enjoyed a relaxed relationship with his valet. Winston had been at his side for a decade, since Ambrose had been a young, angry second son of twenty, carousing his way through Town. And later, when he'd inherited the title from his wastrel brother along with a mountain of debt, Winston had been there to help him navigate the troubled waters of grief and responsibility. Ambrose was thirty now, but he wasn't sure he felt any wiser than the wayward rogue he'd once been. After all, no gentleman would have bedded an innocent at a house party last night as he had.

He knew a pang of guilt for his actions, if not regret.

"As you know, I have become…betrothed to Lady Clementine," he said with care, for although he shared a comfortable friendship with his valet, he had not confided the full truth of his feigned betrothal.

"I'm aware of your betrothal, sir, and I do believe I offered my felicitations? If not, it was unbearably remiss of me, and I must beg your pardon."

"You did, and we both know it, Winston."

His valet remained silent as he scraped the razor along Ambrose's cheek.

"Here is the problem," he began, careful to avoid moving his lips too much as he struggled to find the right words. After a pause, he cleared his throat and began again. "Ahem. The betrothal was made rather in jest. Neither of us had any intention of seeing it to fruition."

"A lark, sir?" Winston finished shaving him and began applying the cooling solution he had concocted himself for just such a purpose.

The man was a wizard, Ambrose was convinced.

But not even the pleasant effect of the post-shaving solution could assuage the turmoil within him. "Of sorts, perhaps. However, I begin to find the notion of taking Lady Clementine as my bride rather appealing."

"Why should you not, my lord?" Winston asked with the same impeccable sangfroid he always possessed. "Lady Clementine hails from an excellent family, she is lovely and accomplished, and by all accounts—forgive me my candor—her dowry is impressive."

Ambrose stroked his smooth jaw and frowned at his reflection in the looking glass Winston had positioned for him to review his results. The valet busied himself with tidying the shaving tools, cleansing and organizing them with efficient movements that bore evidence to the years he had spent in service.

Yes, these were all pragmatic arguments for a union between himself and Clementine. Excellent reasons for making her his marchioness.

"I'm gratified you can see the wisdom in my decision," he said. "However, I fear the lady may not be so inclined."

When he'd left her chamber that morning, she'd been soundly sleeping, curled against him rather like a kitten, and he'd hated leaving her. But he also hadn't wished to disturb her slumber. As a result, no words of a future had been spoken between them.

"And why should she not be, sir?" Winston asked mildly, still toiling about.

He winced. "I'm afraid we haven't always agreed on matters."

Indeed, they hadn't agreed on much aside from the scorching attraction between them.

"I daresay it's customary for men and women in love to disagree," Winston told him sagely. "Quite common, in fact."

Love? He jolted at the notion. Surely not. No, what he felt for her was decidedly not that finer emotion. Was it?

"Have you ever been in love?" he asked his valet, suddenly curious.

"I was, once," Winston said, finishing up his task.

"What happened?" he asked, wondering why, for all their easy camaraderie, he had never spoken with his valet about something of such a personal nature before this morning.

"She fell ill before we could marry," his valet answered, a distinct note of sadness underlying his ordinarily imperturbable voice.

"I'm sorry," Ambrose said instantly, feeling guilty for dredging up Winston's painful past. And feeling guiltier for never having known such a loss had occurred. "Has it happened since you have been with me?"

"No, sir," Winston said with a sad smile. "It was long ago now. Twelve years."

"We need not speak of it further, Winston," he said, not wishing to stir more memories or cause his valet sadness and hurt.

"I don't mind speaking of her," his valet surprised him by saying. "In some ways, it is quite lovely to remember. I often wonder what would have happened had she not gone... However, I'm happy in my position here with you, my lord. The distraction of performing my duties has been appreciated daily."

"If you don't mind, Winston, how did you know you were in love?" he asked slowly, struggling to make sense of his situation, of his valet's unexpected revelations, of *life*, complicated and bloody confusing as it was.

His valet smiled wistfully. "She was all I could think about. When I woke in the morning, all day as I went about my tasks, before I fell asleep at night. It was always her. I couldn't envision myself with anyone else. But that was all a very long time ago, of course, and I shouldn't wish to give in to maudlin sentiment."

It was always her.

Ambrose nodded solemnly. "I understand. Thank you for your honesty, Winston. You've helped me more than you know."

~

"Thank you all so very much for joining me this morning," Vivi announced to the assemblage of ladies the next morning, just after the breakfast Clementine had missed because she had slept through it. "As you know, we've gathered here at Sherborne Manor for a cause most worthy, and whilst I have many entertainments in store for you, each of them pales in comparison to the true importance of our joining together for a common good. To that end, Lady Josephine, I invite you to speak to our little coterie about the Lady's Suffrage Society."

Lady Josephine Decker was dark-haired and lovely, and she was wildly in love with her husband, the famed businessman Elijah Decker, who had accompanied her to the house party. She was also one of the leading members of the Lady's Suffrage Society. Clementine counted her a trusted friend, and she couldn't help but be envious of that lady's husband's clear and utter devotion to her.

"Thank you for the gracious opportunity, Your Grace," Lady Jo said warmly as she rose from her seat and replaced Vivi at the front of the drawing room where a number of the ladies had assembled. "I hope those of you who aren't already members of our cause will consider joining us. As you may know, our most recent efforts to petition the House of Lords to support the bill for women's suffrage failed. However, we won't be discouraged, nor will we relent. Now more than ever, we must continue to pursue the enfranchisement of all, regardless of sex."

Clementine wholeheartedly agreed with all those sentiments. She believed firmly in the voting rights of women, and she hated that her sex had been struggling fruitlessly for decades to achieve the same rights afforded men. She tried to concentrate on Lady Jo, who was a captivating orator in her own right. Clementine wanted to listen, wanted to fill her heart with righteous fury and stand with the ladies who had come to the drawing room and raise a huzzah.

But as she sat flanked by Lady Edith—who had somehow slipped from her dragon mama's watchful eye—and Charity, Clementine's mind inevitably wandered to the reason for the tenderness between her legs. The reason she was so tired. The reason she'd slept straight through breakfast and had scarcely managed to rush into the drawing room at the prescribed time.

Ambrose.

He'd made love to her not once last night but twice, tending to her with gentle care in between, until they'd finally fallen asleep tangled in each other's arms close to dawn. He had somehow slipped unseen from her chamber before her lady's maid had entered that morning, and she'd awoken to an empty bed and rumpled bedclothes that still smelled faintly of him, Oakley looming over her to quietly inform her she'd return later. Clementine was sure she'd been red as a beet and looked guiltier than a bawd in a church pew, but she had been relieved for her lady's maid to take her leave.

She'd felt wicked and yet too tired to bother rising to hide her hastily discarded nightgown or to make certain Ambrose had retrieved all his scattered buttons. Still exhausted, she'd promptly fallen back asleep, body still humming with delightful sensation, only to wake again with a jolt of alarm, the ticking mantel clock telling her she'd missed breakfast and was about to miss Vivi's meeting for the Lady's Suffrage Society.

Guilt seeped through her. She wondered if she looked different. Could anyone tell what she'd been about the night before? Had Oakley suspected? If so, the loyal lady's maid hadn't spoken a word of her concerns as she had plaited Clementine's hair in a Grecian braid. Did her friends suspect?

She slanted a glance in Charity's direction and caught her dear friend's gaze. Charity raised her golden brows and mouthed something Clementine couldn't discern. Which was just as well. She wouldn't dream of whispering during Lady Jo's stirring speech. She shook her head and turned her attention back to the front of the brightly lit drawing room.

But once more, her mind whirled. Had her absence at breakfast been remarked upon? She hoped not, for it was an informal affair, Vivi having arranged for the sideboard to be eternally stocked for the morning hours, guests free to come and go as they pleased. But what if someone had seen Ambrose sneak from her chamber? What if they were forced to marry in truth?

It astonished her to realize that such a fate didn't seem nearly as daunting and terrible as it had not long ago. Except, the tender new feelings she was harboring for Ambrose were foolish, weren't they? For the second time, she had fallen for a rake with a rake's handsome face and a rake's easy, seductive wiles. A rake who had spoken not one word of making an honest woman of her. No, indeed, he'd only spoken of leaving today.

Good heavens.

She felt the blood draining from her face, panic making her stomach seize.

Surely he wasn't leaving today. Was he? A fine sheen of sweat broke out on her brow, and she opened her fan, waving it in an effort to cool herself. Her corset was laced too tightly. She could scarcely breathe.

What if she swooned?

What if Ambrose had already left?

"Psst," Charity hissed, drawing Clementine's gaze. "Do I need to fetch the hartshorn?" she whispered.

"I'm not going to swoon," she muttered as quietly as she could from behind her fan.

"You look as if you are," her friend countered.

"Someone is going to swoon?" Lady Edith murmured.

"No," she said succinctly.

"Tiny is," Charity said at the same time.

"We're meant to be paying attention to Lady Jo," she grumbled, grateful they were seated near the rear of the drawing room where they couldn't serve as an interruption to her friend.

"I'm sure Lady Jo wouldn't wish for you to swoon," Lady Edith countered sensibly. "Do you need some air?"

What she needed was to know if Ambrose had left. To know if anyone had seen him leaving her chamber. To berate herself for giving in to her inner wickedness. For somehow allowing a rake into her heart, knowing how futile and painful doing so would be.

Rakes.

What beastly, monstrous, insidious, thoroughly wretched creatures they were.

"I'm merely a trifle warm," she said flatly, fanning herself. "Do let us listen."

That silenced her friends for the moment. The Countess

of Sinclair was next to speak, followed by Lady Huntingdon. The rest of the meeting unfolded at a torpid pace, until Clementine almost couldn't bear another moment of remaining seated, swimming in misery now that the glow of passion had firmly receded.

She'd made a mistake.

A dreadful one.

She couldn't possibly be in love with the Marquess of Dorset. Could she? Surely she was all wrong about her feelings. After all, she scarcely knew him. Love couldn't come upon one so swiftly. What she was feeling instead was likely physical rather than emotional. The aftereffects of all the pleasure Ambrose had visited upon her.

Yes, that was all it was. And he had been correct last night. He needed to leave, but first, they would end their engagement. It would be in both their best interests, for it was plain as the nose on her face that they would never suit. Not in any way, save one, and as wondrous as last night had been, she couldn't afford to risk near-ruin again.

The gentle round of feminine applause alerted her to the conclusion of the meeting. Ladies rose from their seats, shaking out their skirts, gathering to sign their names to a new petition. Clementine flew from her seat as if it had been fashioned of flame, and it may as well have been for how overheated she was. Vivi joined them, smiling and looking effortlessly elegant as always.

"My dears," she said. "What did you think of the talk?"

"It was wonderful," Clementine said, though in truth, she'd scarcely heard a word of it.

"Very persuasive," Lady Edith added. "I thoroughly enjoyed every word. I must thank you for making certain my mother was otherwise occupied this morning."

Vivi's smile deepened, turning into a mischievous grin.

"You needn't thank me, dearest. Such is the role of the dutiful hostess."

"I'd like to add my signature to the petition," Lady Edith said firmly, shoulders going back.

It was a moment of true rebellion, and Clementine would have applauded her new friend for her bravery had she not been swimming in a sea of uncertainty.

"Wonderful," Vivi said. "Lady Jo has them just over here. Come, let us all go and add our names."

"Wait," Charity said, staying their small group's motion toward the gaggle of ladies adding their signatures at the opposite end of the drawing room. "Something is amiss. Tiny, you look as if you are holding in something dreadful. Out with it, if you please."

Clementine took a deep breath, making certain there were no other ladies within earshot.

"I am going to have to cry off my engagement to Lord Dorset," she announced. "Today."

Vivi frowned. "That was remarkably short-lived, but then you did say it was temporary."

"Quite," she said miserably. "Our betrothal is a pretense because of the bee incident."

So why, then, did part of her yearn for something more?

"Because Dorset was found beneath your skirts." Charity flashed a saucy smirk.

Clementine's cheeks went hot. "He was not beneath my skirts."

Yes, he had been. And quite thoroughly, too. Last night, most recently. Her ears felt as if they were on fire, and she averted her gaze.

"He was a bit," Lady Edith countered.

"Are your ears flushing?" Charity asked, sounding intrigued.

"Indeed, they are," Vivi said.

"My ears are not flushing," she countered, though they did feel as scorching as her cheeks.

"You're positively aflame, Tiny," Charity offered.

"Charity," she growled, feeling quite uncharitable toward her free-spirited friend. "You're disconcerting me in a most disagreeable fashion."

"Come now, Clementine," Vivi soothed. "You know Charity is always disconcerting."

"I shall consider that a compliment," Charity said, grinning.

"You don't seem happy about this development, Lady Clementine," Lady Edith observed, frowning. "Did you want to marry the marquess after all?"

"Not at all," she lied hastily. "I am quite happy to end this farce. Relieved, in fact. Truly."

"My dear, what is that mark on your neck?" Charity asked, peering at Clemetine's throat.

Her hand flew to cover the spot. "What mark?"

How had she not taken note when she had looked at her reflection this morning? But then, had she truly looked at herself? She'd been at sixes and sevens, praying Oakley wouldn't ask unwanted questions or take note of anything untoward.

"Oh no," Vivi said.

Charity chuckled. "Tiny, you scoundrel."

Oh, this was truly terrible. Her mortification knew no end, which only seemed to heighten Charity's enjoyment of the situation.

"Women aren't scoundrels," she said weakly.

"Nonsense," Lady Edith countered. "Of course they are. I once had a trusted friend who proved a dreadful one. Naturally, she's no longer my friend."

There was a story there, but Clementine would pursue it later. For now, she was more concerned with the potential scandal brewing. A scandal which she had to squelch at all costs.

"Please don't breathe a word of this to your mother," she entreated her newest friend.

"I would never dream of telling her anything I wouldn't want all the world to know," Lady Edith reassured her gently.

"Are you certain you truly want to end your betrothal, Tiny?" Charity asked, perceptive as always beneath the façade of outrageousness she perpetually donned.

"Of course I do," she said hastily. "Dorset is a rake. He has no more wish to marry me than I do him."

But she was protesting too much, and she knew it. The claims rang false even to her own ears.

"Then why do you seem so miserable at the prospect?" Charity asked softly.

"Oh, my dear," Vivi breathed before she could answer. "You're in love with him, aren't you?"

"Of course not," Clementine denied. "I don't even *like* him. I scarcely know him."

But a voice inside her, one she had been doing her utmost to ignore, reminded her that was not entirely true. The marquess had undeniably ingratiated himself to her over the course of the house party. He had carried her in his arms all the way to her chamber when she'd been stung. And had he not caught her, keeping her from injuring herself in the library when she had lost her balance and fallen from the ladder? To say nothing of his kindness in the gardens, or the way he made her melt whenever he so much as looked in her direction.

She didn't dislike him. In fact, she liked him very much. Oh God. She *did* love him. That terrible, rakish, handsome rogue had cast a spell over her with his kisses and his sinful mouth, and his...*everything else*, and now she was thoroughly trapped.

Lady Edith, Charity, and Vivi were watching her, their countenances suggesting they didn't believe a word of her disavowal.

"Tiny," Charity said, giving her arm a comforting squeeze. "It seems as if the matchmaker has finally found a match of her own."

"What shall we do about it?" Lady Edith asked.

Vivi smiled. "I have a plan."

CHAPTER 12

Clementine slanted a glance in Dorset's direction as they fell into step behind the rest of the small group that had been assembled at Vivi's prompting following the Lady's Suffrage Society meeting. He hadn't left Sherborne Manor, much to her relief. Not yet, anyway. But neither had he sought her out. She had no notion of what he was thinking, what to expect from him.

And it quite terrified her.

She'd been at the mercy of a rake before, and it had left her heart dashed to bits.

Still, she couldn't help but to admire how devilishly handsome he was this late morning, the slashing prominence of his clean-shaven jaw calling for her hand and lips, his sensual mouth making her long for more kisses.

He cocked his head to the side suddenly as if sensing her regard, his stare—a shade of verdant green to rival the vibrant, grassy knoll upon which they strolled—meshing with hers. "I must apologize," he told her, his voice low.

The tentative hope inside her began to crack like an egg. Ahead of them, Vivi, Lady Edith, the Misses Chartrand,

Charity, and Viscount Wilton were walking at a discreet distance, though near enough to eavesdrop if their voices were to carry. She allowed her steps to slow a bit more, widening the gap and providing them more privacy.

"Why must you apologize?" she asked him guardedly, her voice equally quiet and cautious as she cast another glance in his direction.

He frowned. "I paid you a dishonor yesterday, and that was never my intention."

Also not what she wanted to hear. Oh, it wasn't as if she had been expecting a declaration of eternal love, but after the passionate night they'd shared, and after her realizations that morning, she'd been stupidly hoping for something far more than an apology.

"It was badly done of both of us," she allowed coolly as they walked toward the River Derwent, which ran through Sherborne Manor. Clinging to her pride seemed the wisest path at the moment; the ardent lover who had arrived at her door in the darkest depths of the night was nowhere to be found now.

"It never should have happened," he told her, and everything inside her froze.

So that was to be the way of it, then. Of course it was. Had she expected differently of him? Everything between them had been a sham thus far. Last night had been nothing more than an aberration for him. She'd been a convenient vessel for his lust.

Clementine's stomach gave a violent surge. She wanted to retch. Or to hit him with something. But they were in the midst of the outdoors, and they had no weapons readily available.

Hold your head high, she told herself. *You've been here before. Do not let him see how deeply affected you are.*

"It was a dreadful mistake," she forced out, her voice

strained. "We're fortunate indeed that we are not marrying in truth. The two of us would never suit."

"No?" he asked lightly, keeping his face averted to the path ahead of them and giving her no hint of what he was thinking. "I rather think we suit in some ways."

Heat washed over Clementine, her body throbbing in unwanted remembrance of just how thoroughly they had suited each other in the library. In her bedroom. But he had apologized for what had been the most transcendent moment of her life. Had said it never should have happened. How dare he throw her reaction to his seduction in her face now?

"We must put an end to our betrothal," she said curtly, for it was the only answer. "Immediately. We can inform everyone on this walk that we have changed our minds, and when we return to the house, we can make a formal announcement to all."

"You are eager to sever our agreement," he pointed out, his frown deepening. "After last night—"

"Why would I not be?" she interrupted, almost unable to bear another crushing word from him. "Far better to put an end to this nonsense before we take it any further."

"Nonsense," he repeated, his baritone taking on a new tone.

"How else to describe it? No need to inflict more misery upon ourselves than we already have. It is plain as the clouds in the sky overhead that we loathe each other."

"It did not feel as if you loathed me last night," he said, slanting her a knowing look. "But then, perhaps it's just as well, for I have no wish to marry at all, let alone chain myself to someone so inconstant."

The utter bastard. How dare he call her inconstant when he was the heartless rake? Was that his game then, lure her neatly into his trap, and once it was sprung, taunt her with how easily she'd been ensnared?

"I would have reacted the same way with any gentleman," she lied.

"Oh?" He stopped and turned toward her. "And how many other gentlemen have you been welcoming into your bed?"

None, of course, and he knew it.

She was forced to stop and face him as well. The rest of the party was far ahead of them by now, beyond earshot. If any of them thought it was odd that Clementine and Dorset were lingering behind, squaring off like a pair of prize-fighters preparing for a bout, they gave no indication. No one even cast a glance in their direction.

She jerked her attention back to the tall, handsome, glowering male before her.

"As my former betrothed, it is hardly any of your concern whether or not I choose to welcome others into my bed in the future," she informed him icily. "Indeed, I must thank you for opening my eyes to a world which I'd been previously missing."

"Damn it, Clementine, there won't be any others," he growled.

She tipped up her chin and pinned him with a glare. "Of course there will. Why shouldn't there be? I'm a thoroughly modern lady. Free to do as I wish, with whomever I wish it."

A muscle in his jaw had begun to tick. "Over my dead and bloodied carcass, you will."

She was about to respond when a commotion rose from the direction of the group gathered by the river.

"Something must be amiss," she said needlessly.

From their vantage point on the knoll overlooking the River Derwent, Clementine could clearly see Charity waving her arms, Lady Edith pointing, and Miss Madeline Chartrand pressing a hand to her mouth as the others looked into the waters.

"Come," Dorset said, voice grim as he took her hand in his and began hauling her toward the river.

∽

THE SOURCE of the alarm became apparent as Ambrose and Clementine reached the riverbank.

A tiny, furred creature was bobbing in the current, heading downstream.

"A kitten has fallen into the water," Lady Charity announced. "Wilton can't swim. Can you?"

"I can." Ambrose was already shedding his blasted coat, feeling grimmer than he had to begin with, when Clementine had been stomping roughshod all over his attempts at a bloody proposal.

"You must save the poor darling," one of the Miss Chartrands urged.

He was having a devil of a time recalling which of them was which.

"I'll do my best." He took off his shoes and hat.

"Are you a strong swimmer?" Clementine asked, her lovely countenance marked with what he would have sworn was concern had she not just so thoroughly eviscerated him up there on the knoll.

"I excel at swimming," he told her coolly. "Not that you ought to care."

With that parting shot, he stalked down the riverbank and waded in. The water was cool, the rocks beneath his feet slippery. The kitten was bobbing ever farther downstream, and there was not a moment to waste. Finding his way in the current, he waded deeper until he could float, and from there, it was just a matter of propelling himself with as much speed as possible. He stroked through the water, determined. The cheers of the ladies on the bank spurred him on.

He was gaining on the pathetic little creature, whose small legs were no match for the current. The poor fellow was paddling, his head just above the water, nothing more than a scrap of drenched orange fur.

Dorset stroked and kicked. Finally, he reached the kitten and caught him by the scruff of his neck. Now came the truly difficult part of this rescue—swimming back to the bank with one arm as he held the kitten above the water with the other. Slowly, painstakingly, he made his way to the bank. After what seemed an eternity but must have been mere minutes, he reached a part of the river where he could stand. Cuddling the terrified creature to his chest, he emerged, sloshing through the water.

The ladies of the party were applauding him as if he'd just won a war. But as he held the trembling kitten to his chest and slogged through the grassy riverbank, he had eyes for only one woman.

The woman who had just told him she wanted to end their betrothal immediately.

It was a dreadful mistake. The two of us would never suit.

Her taunting words echoed in his mind, resonating. Mocking. Troubling. He wished he could read her gaze from this distance. Wished he could do something more than stand there on the banks of the blasted River Derwent, dripping like a fish freshly plucked from the waters. But he could not, because something strange had settled over him. A kind of mental torpor.

There in the summer sun, as he stood soaked to the skin, a bedraggled kitten's fierce claws cutting into his chest, he made the most astonishing, horrifying, bloody terrible realization.

He loved Lady Clementine Hammond.

The kitten, now freed of the water and no longer in imminent danger, began attempting to climb him like a damned tree. He wondered if he was bleeding. The pain searing his chest suggested he was.

But he was too flummoxed to care.

He was *in love* with the most maddening baggage he had ever met. With the meddlesome woman responsible for Anna throwing him over. With the last woman he should have found himself drawn to at this cursed house party. With the only lady who had been foolish enough to gallivant without her drawers in the midst of a garden and managed to get a bee up her skirts. With the woman who had brought him to his knees last night, only to tell him to go to the devil this morning.

The kitten sank its claws into the sensitive patch of skin between his neck and shoulder, digging in as if attempting to punish Dorset for its adventure in the river. Or as if attempting to crawl inside his damned body. He patted the creature, trying to calm it. There was hope for the thing yet, and mayhap, just mayhap, for himself and Clementine as well.

~

THE MARQUESS OF DORSET had emerged from the river like some sort of mythic god. His white shirt was soaked and clung lovingly to every contour of his well-muscled chest. His trousers were stuck to his thick horseman's thighs and calves. Although his dark hair was slicked to his head, he looked nothing short of glorious. Disturbingly masculine.

And he had saved a kitten, which took the opportunity to burrow its tiny self into his neck. Using claws, if his sudden grimace was any indication. But he remained gentle and tender, slowly stroking the orange kitten's back with his large hand.

She wanted to hate him, but how could she when she loved the miserable man so?

"He rescued the kitten," Charity said on a dramatic sigh as if reading Clementine's thoughts, pressing a hand to her heart. "Oh, Tiny, I am *in love*."

"With the creature or with the Marquess of Dorset?" Wilton asked stiffly from Charity's other side. "Either way, I daresay your affections are appallingly easily won, Lady Charity."

Charity sent the proper viscount a minx's grin. "Is that jealousy I detect in your voice, my lord?"

Wilton scoffed. "Jealousy is an emotion that is both futile and puerile."

Clementine looked from the rigid viscount to her wild friend, wondering at their exchange but unable to make sense of anything more than immediate facts.

The kitten.

It had been adrift in the River Derwent.

Now saved.

The Marquess of Dorset's vibrant, emerald gaze upon her.

The beating of her heart.

The warmth of the sun.

The strong slash of his jaw, the perfectly molded sculpture of his lips.

His tender passion last night.

The yearning inside her.

Nothing made sense, and yet, everything did.

Dorset was stalking toward her. His eyes on her. He was drenched. And handsome. So very handsome. And...

Bleeding.

He stopped before her, towering over her with his greater

height. The kitten's sharp claws had punctured his flesh. Small dots of crimson blood stained his shirt over his heart and trickled down his throat to his necktie, where the kitten had climbed.

"My lord," she said breathlessly. "You're injured."

"The bloody feline is attempting to slay the very man who saved it from a watery death," he said, still petting the soaked orange fur.

"Would you like me to take the kitten?" she asked, thinking she ought to aid him in some way. "Those claws look painful."

"If you can dislodge it from my neck, I would be most appreciative," he said.

And how strange that they were speaking civilly, when not half an hour before, they had been cutting each other down and delivering verbal barbs as painful as the kitten's claws. But she was the one he approached when he was dripping and bleeding.

He had come to her.

She stepped nearer, forgetting they had an audience until Vivi and Lady Edith appeared at her shoulder.

"Pinch the kitten's neck as her mother would do," Lady Edith advised, her tone no-nonsense. "Then gently remove her paws from Lord Dorset's neck."

"The poor darling was floating in the river when we neared the bank," Vivi said. "Who knows how long she had been floating or where she fell in. She must have been terrified."

"I wonder where her mama is," Charity cooed. "What a darling little beast. Oh, look at all that orange fur."

"I hate to offer opposition, but I am reasonably certain the furred beggar is a male," Dorset said wryly. "Most cats with his coloring are."

"It hardly matters if he is a male or a female cat," Clementine said, attempting to dislodge the kitten as Lady Edith had instructed. "You are a hero, Lord Dorset. You saved him."

Their gazes clashed and held for one soul-searing moment. "It was nothing," he said.

She turned her attention back to the kitten, extricating him from Dorset's poor neck and bringing his tiny body to her bosom to cradle him against her.

"It was most certainly not *nothing* as you suggested," she told Dorset. "And you are soaked. You'll contract a lung infection."

"Careful, my lady, or I shall convince myself that is concern I hear in your voice."

There was no mistaking the wryness in his tone.

"Of course I was concerned," she told him quietly before thinking better of the words.

Ambrose—*Dorset*, she corrected herself—had been nothing short of magnificent, rushing into the water to save such a small life. And there was no doubt in her mind that if he had not rescued the kitten now clinging to her bodice, his sharp claws digging through her layers and burrowing into her corset, that the poor thing would have been swept downstream to his death. Perhaps there lived a small, shriveled heart after all, somewhere within his sleek, rakish shell.

"We were *all* concerned," Charity said into the awkward silence that had fallen following Clementine's stupid words. "You are, just as Tiny said, a hero, Lord Dorset. The kitten would never have survived if you had not risked yourself to save her."

"Tiny?" Dorset asked, raising a brow.

"My sobriquet for Lady Clementine," Charity explained, giving Clementine a surreptitious wink.

Lovely. Thank you for your help, Charity.

All she needed was for the Marquess of Dorset to begin calling her Tiny. Clementine sent her friend a pointed look.

But Charity was already gazing in Viscount Wilton's direction once more. Interesting, that. They seemed true opposites. Clementine was sure his lordship would swallow his tongue if he ever discovered Charity preferred to eschew her drawers in the summer months. And that she had kissed a footman—with tongue—when she was fifteen. And that she had posed nearly nude for a portrait...

"Ah," was all the marquess said, before casting a look around him at the riverbank, where he had abandoned his shoes, coat, and waistcoat before rushing into the river.

"You are indeed the gentleman of the hour," Wilton drawled, before securing Dorset's discarded garments and handing them to him.

"It was nothing," Dorset repeated as a sudden gust of wind tore through the river valley.

The wind was rather chilly, and it left Clementine feeling cool despite the sun. She could only imagine what Dorset must be experiencing, drenched as he was.

"We should all return to Sherborne Manor," Clementine said, still cradling the kitten, her eyes lingering upon the marquess.

But he studiously avoided her gaze.

CHAPTER 13

In the span of a morning, Clementine had lost one betrothed and gained one kitten. For it seemed that the small scrap of fur now considered her his new mother. They had returned to Sherborne Manor with a dripping Dorset, who had been hailed as a hero by the rest of the guests—even Lady Featherstone had grudgingly conceded his efforts had been most dashing. Clementine had brought the kitten to her chamber, where she had dried him off and offered him a bowl of meat sent up from the kitchens. He had tucked into his luncheon promptly.

And now, he was settled comfortably on her lap, sleeping away. Either he had not been a wild kitten and was accustomed to people, or the food offering had persuaded him that Clementine was trustworthy. She was amused by his sudden docile nature, but she supposed the poor fellow had suffered quite an ordeal.

She had settled in the window seat in her guest chamber, which overlooked a portion of the gardens. The day beyond her windowpane was bright and cheerful, the lush glory of the gardens most inviting. But although she had found the nook charming upon her arrival, and though the sweetly sleeping kitten nestled on her lap was a source of comfort, Clementine could not seem to stop her mind from wandering to thoughts of *him*.

A knock sounded on her chamber door just then.

"Come," she called, assuming it was one of her friends.

Likely Charity, who had taken quite a liking to the kitten, even if she did insist upon referring to the feline as a *she*.

The door opened, and Clementine could not have been more shocked by the person crossing the threshold and closing the portal quickly behind lest anyone in the hall see.

"Ambrose," she exclaimed.

Then cursed herself for the slip and the familiarity both.

He had changed out of his river-sodden clothes, she noted as he sauntered across the chamber. His dark hair was wavy and tousled, the ends still looking a bit damp. But aside from that lingering sign of his swim in the River Derwent, he was impeccably groomed in country tweed, a crisp white shirt, and a gray waistcoat that somehow managed to magnify the brilliance of his gaze.

"What are you doing in my chamber?" she blurted next.

He stopped near enough to touch. Near enough for temptation.

"I came to check on the scamp I saved from the river," he said softly, his gaze traveling over her face as if he intended to commit it to memory.

"Our little friend is fine, as you can see," she said, directing a pointed glance to her lap, where the kitten blinked drowsily and then continued to sleep. "If that is all you wanted, you might have sent a note or one of the other ladies in attendance to check on him. You cannot be alone with me in my room. Once was more than perilous enough."

"It's scandalous of me, I know," he said.

And yet, he made no move to go. Nor did he appear particularly contrite.

Blast the man. Why did he have to smell so good? Ought he not to stink of fish and mud after his adventure in the river?

She frowned at him, thinking him unbearably exasperating. "We have only just decided to end our betrothal. It would hardly do for you to be discovered here."

"As I recall, we had yet to complete our discussion concerning the betrothal," he said, bending down to give the kitten's back a tender stroke.

As he did so, their bare fingers brushed.

Everything within her seized. Her heart, her breath. Although she knew she must not, she glanced up at him, only to discover their faces were devastatingly near. His lips were close enough to set hers upon them.

She swallowed. "I believed our conversation was complete, Lord Dorset."

"Dorset, am I?" he said, giving her one of his most charming grins, the sort that made the corners of his eyes crinkle. "When I first entered, you called me Ambrose."

So she had.

"How unkind of you to take note and remind me," she grumbled.

His thumb rubbed slow circles over her inner wrist. And the effect that small gesture had upon her was no different than it had been the previous occasion he had caressed her thus. Her insides were melting.

So much inner frenzy and furor, all from a mere thumb.

"Why unkind?" he asked softly.

His gaze was intent, and she felt it all the way to her toes, that something special that happened to her whenever he was near.

"Because I was too familiar, and I should not have been."

"I think we have been too familiar with each other from the first." His hand covered hers, resting upon the slumbering kitten. "Besides, I rather like when you're familiar with me, darling."

The look he cast her way was laden with such tenderness. Her foolish heart leapt.

But no. Surely she was imagining it?

"It's hardly gentlemanly of you to say such a thing," she said tartly, trying to keep her guard firmly in place.

"Have you not learned by now?" A wicked grin curved his sensual lips. "I am no gentleman. Not where you're concerned."

"A rakehell through and through," she said, trying to keep the breathlessness from her voice.

The grin slid from his mouth. "What if I could be reformed? By the right lady, of course?"

"What are you suggesting, Lord Dorset?"

"After I returned from our walk and had a chance to calm my anger, I had an astonishing realization."

What was this?

Calm down, heart. You shall get us into a great deal of trouble if you do not cease this nonsense.

"Oh?" She was careful to keep her features calm. To show none of the sudden upheaval within her.

"I realized I was wrong."

She waited for him to say more, as everything within her tensed as tightly as a freshly wound watch spring. But he was silent, his expression implacable as he watched her.

"And what is it you were wrong about?" she prodded when she could bear the silence no longer.

"About getting married."

That was not precisely what she had wanted to hear.

"To anyone, or have you a specific lady in mind?"

"Oh no. I could not marry just anyone," he said, resuming

those maddening circles of his, this time on the back of her hand. "It would have to be a very specific lady, indeed."

She clenched her jaw. "I wish you happy, then. You may thank me for setting you free, all the better to pursue her."

Her heart, which had been floating with premature happiness, was suddenly heavy as a boulder, threatening to crush her beneath its weight. Blinking against a furious rush of tears, she jerked her attention to the window. Beyond the panes, the bright, beckoning Yorkshire countryside blurred.

What was wrong with her? How had she been so reckless, so careless, as to fall in love with a charming rake like the Marquess of Dorset? She had known from the moment he had announced their betrothal that it was a sham. And she had not liked him. Nor had she wanted to marry him.

Why had he made her fall in love with him?

Just as she had believed, her fate was to remain forever alone. Her heart was destined to be broken.

"Clementine."

She swallowed. "Why are you still here, Dorset? Have you not a bride to be wooing?"

"Will you not look at me? This is bloody difficult enough without you staring out the cursed window as if you cannot bear the sight of me."

His low rumble had her turning back to him. "She will no doubt be easily won since you have been hailed as the hero of the house party."

If there was bitterness in her voice, it could not be helped. The notion of Ambrose flirting with, charming, kissing another lady. Of offering to marry that lady instead, hurt.

"I hope she will be," he said earnestly, "though she has not proven easily won thus far. Indeed, she has led me on a merry chase. She has also told me we would never suit and that she does not like me. How shall I change her mind, do you suppose? Was the kitten rescue sufficient?"

She blinked. He could not be speaking of *her*, could he? "You are confusing me, Dorset. Cease speaking in riddles."

"You, Clementine," he said, the tenderness once more creeping into his expression. "You are the woman I wish to marry. I knew it this morning, I knew it last night. I knew it when I stood on the banks of the River Derwent, sodden to the bone, this little puff of fur attempting to assassinate me with his claws. I had eyes only for you. You were all I wanted to see. Somewhere along the way, our ruse has ceased to be a fiction for me. I can only hope that you may be willing to reconsider throwing me over. When we had that row just before we were called to the river, and you told me you wanted to end our betrothal immediately, it changed me. *You* changed me."

Her heart was racing as if she had just run to the River Derwent anew. Her mind was swirling. She could not seem to make sense of what Ambrose had just said to her.

"You want to marry me," she repeated.

The kitten, either sensing the heaviness of the emotions around him or growing weary of the pair of hands atop his small back, shifted and yawned. Dorset retracted his hand, and so did she, allowing the little orange cat to shift until he was content.

"I do," he said.

"But you blame me for the Marchioness of Huntly marrying the marquess and throwing you over," she protested stupidly.

Why am I protesting?

I want to marry him too, do I not?

"I did blame you," he admitted, then winced. "Damnation, but this is a deuced awkward position. Do you mind if I join you on the seat?"

The seat was generous in size, and there was ample room for him. Clementine shifted her rump to the left, disturbing her lap-dweller in the process. The kitten blinked sleepily up at her and mewed.

"I am sorry, little fellow," she crooned to him.

As if he understood, the kitten shifted against her, settling into a new position that was to his liking. But in the next moment, she forgot all about the kitten in her lap.

The marquess folded his tall, lean form onto the cushion at her side. His hip was pressed to hers, his warmth invading her through all the layers of civility separating her bare skin from his.

How strange it was, she thought, the barriers of clothing. Fashioned to hide the body, to protect modesty, and yet cleverly contrived in a way to put as much of the body on display as possible. In Dorset, it was his broad shoulders filling out his coat, his long legs encased in tweed trousers. It was the bare skin of his neck and jaw, the masculine protrusion of his Adam's apple above the simple necktie he wore. It was his hands, the fingers long and strong, the nails neat.

His beautiful face, hovering so near to hers.

His lips.

"We should name him," he said.

Her mind was as blank as a new sheet of paper.

"I beg your pardon?"

"The kitten who has decided you are his mama," he clarified, that beautiful grin of his returning. "He ought to have a name, do you not think?"

The Marquess of Dorset excelled at stealing her breath. And making her long for him.

"Have you a recommendation?" she asked, silently congratulating herself for neither allowing her voice to tremble nor hauling him to her for a greedy, elated, relieved kiss.

"Fergus," he said.

"You think he is Scottish?"

"I think he has the red hair of a Scot." Dorset winked. "And I also think the idea of having an orange cat named Fergus following us about at Tildon Court pleases me."

Tildon Court.

His country seat.

"You never did tell me about it," she said, recalling their earlier conversation.

"A pile of rubble," he responded with the same lack of concern he had earlier evinced. "A draughty old tumbledown castle that is largely uninhabitable unless you are a bloody mouse. There was a fire some years ago, which I daresay did not help matters. But still, the park is lovely. A lake lies within, along with forest and verdant fields. There is a river as well, though I cannot say whether we shall find any kittens floating within it."

"It sounds lovely. I adore castles."

Dorset shrugged. "If one likes draughts and mice and dust and despicable lighting. To say nothing of crumbling ruins."

Old castles, crumbling or no, sounded intriguing to Clementine. She had always been a lover of history. There was something about the idea of returning Tildon Court to its former glory that appealed to her.

That felt *right*.

Just as the Marquess of Dorset did.

"It hardly sounds as despicable as you would have me believe, my lord," she said softly.

"It was never my intention to suggest my country seat is despicable." He leaned into her, crowding her with his big, masculine body and his seductive scent. "I merely wished to warn you. As the Marchioness of Dorset, the obligations awaiting you would be many."

Was she imagining the wicked gleam in his eyes? She thought not.

"Obligations?" she queried.

"I hope not all of your duties as my wife would be obligatory," he said, voice low and deep and decadent as morning chocolate and the finest silk and the sweetest perfume all at once.

My wife.

Heavens.

"You mean it, then?" she blurted. "You want to marry me?"

"Yes, as I said."

"Did you swallow river water?"

The corners of his lips kicked up. "No."

"Strike your head?"

"No."

She narrowed her eyes. "Are you delirious with fever?"

He pressed a hand to his forehead. "I daresay not. Would you like to feel?"

Yes, she very much would. But she would not stop at his forehead, which meant she needed to keep her hands in her lap where they belonged.

She frowned. This interrogation needed to be complete. "Are you proposing to me because you need my dowry?"

He shook his head slowly. "No, darling. I'll not lie. I'm pockets to let, waist-deep in debt. But I'll happily sell off everything I can to stay afloat, do anything I must. Keep your dowry. All I want is you. Clementine—or shall I call you Tiny?"

"If you do, I shall brain you."

"Lady Charity calls you Tiny," he pointed out.

"Lady Charity also persuaded me it was *de règle* to go about without one's drawers in the summer," she groused before thinking better of her revelation.

But far from being horrified, Dorset appeared amused.

"Indeed?" he asked, after a bark of deep, delightful laughter. "What a pair she would make with Wilton."

"Wilton?" Clementine thought of the very proper viscount and wrinkled her nose. "I do doubt she would have him. He's far too concerned with propriety to be of interest to her."

"Hmm," was all Dorset said, still looking and sounding vastly entertained. "No Tiny, then?"

"You may call me Clementine," she said. "Or any other term of endearment."

"Does that mean you have changed your mind, darling?"

Changed her mind?

For a moment, she was hopelessly confused, until she realized he was referring to their earlier conversation that morning, and what now seemed a lifetime ago, when she had told him she wished to end their betrothal at once.

And then, it occurred to her that he had yet to speak words of love. He had said he wanted to marry her, yes. He had said she had changed him. However, he had not spoken the one four-letter word that would make all the difference to her bruised and battered heart.

Love.

"I am…considering changing my mind," she said.

He grimaced. "That hardly sounds promising."

"What shall we tell the others?" she asked, not wanting to question him directly about love and yet unable to keep from thinking about it.

"We need tell them nothing. As far as they are concerned, we are already betrothed."

"But my friends all know it was a pretense," she countered, determined.

He raised a dark brow. "Will your friends care if we have changed our minds? Do you find them untrustworthy?"

"No, of course not."

"Then we need offer no explanations."

Either he was being obtuse, or love was not a part of his

thoughts when he had made his earlier decision. "What of your feelings for Lady Huntly? Do you still love her?"

"No, I do not. Christ, what a clod I am, going about this proposal all wrong." He ran his fingers through his tousled hair. "The last time I proposed marriage to a lady, we were not already betrothed, nor had she just told me she wished to end our betrothal immediately that morning. I will admit, I have no notion of how to proceed. Then again, look at how that turned out."

The smile on his lips was hesitant and beautiful, and she wanted nothing more than to throw herself into his arms and kiss him until they were both breathless. But two things stopped her. The first was the kitten nestled in her lap. The second was Ambrose himself. While he had conceded with ease that he no longer loved the marchioness, he still had yet to speak any words of love concerning Clementine.

"How can you be so certain I'm the woman for you?" she asked him quietly, searching his gaze, hoping to find the answers she sought there. "It's only been mere days..."

"Do you believe in fate?"

His question took her by surprise, for the Marquess of Dorset had not struck her as a particularly fanciful man.

"I have always thought fate was cruel," she confessed.

She had found Walter, only to be betrayed by him. Was that not the definition of cruelty?

And yet...

She had found the Marquess of Dorset. All thanks to Vivi's house party.

"What if *we* are fate?" he pressed. "You and I? What if we were meant to find each other here in Yorkshire? What if I was always meant to love you?"

There was the word she had been seeking.

Her heart pounded with so much force, she did not doubt he could hear it. "Do you? Love me, that is?"

"Have I not said so before now? You ought to kick me in the arse." He flashed her a wry grin that somehow only served to heighten his magnetism. "I love you, Lady Clementine Hammond. I do not know quite when this madness started, but all I do know is that I want to make you my marchioness in truth. I don't expect you to return my feelings immediately. All I can hope is that, given time, you shall—"

"I do," she blurted.

CHAPTER 14

*A*mbrose blinked. "You do?" he repeated, certain he had misheard.

And if he had not, well then, *by God*, he wanted the words. He needed her declaration. He had to know she felt the same maddening, vexing, foolish, reckless, wonderful emotion galloping through her heart.

She nodded, and for the first time since he had truly come to know Clementine here at Sherborne Manor, she appeared genuinely vulnerable. Hesitant. The shell of perfection she had crafted around herself had cracked. Beneath it was simply the woman she was.

Not the matchmaker.

Not the lady he had resented from afar.

No, indeed.

She was something altogether different. Something rare and wonderful. And he was damn well going to make her his.

As long as she agreed to be his wife, that was.

Which she had not yet.

Damn it.

"I love you too, Ambrose," she said then, chasing his fears in the best possible manner.

He'd come to her with no expectations. Indeed, with nary a hope she would return his feelings.

For a moment, he had no words.

So he did what came naturally.

He lowered his lips to hers and claimed them in a kiss. Her mouth was sweet and soft and responsive as ever. She kissed him back, opening without his needing to coax her, the velvety tip of her tongue sliding sinuously against his. He could not resist cupping her cheek with his hand. Her skin was smooth and warm and vital.

He kissed the corners of her lips, first one and then the other. Kissed her upper lip where the Cupid's bow drove him to distraction. Sucked on the fullness of the lower, nipping it with his teeth, then soothing the sting with his tongue. He kissed a path along her jaw, all the way to her ear.

If he wasn't careful, he was going to haul her into his arms and carry her back to her bed and sink deep inside her.

He kissed the shell of her ear, inhaling the sweet scent of her hair. "Will you marry me, Clementine? Will you be my marchioness?"

"Yes." Her sigh hummed with contentment. "I'll marry you, Ambrose."

He would have kissed her again had not a knock sounded on her door.

They parted hastily, Clementine's cheeks blushing a fetching shade of pink. He was briefly mesmerized by the sight of her.

Mine, he thought, feeling a bit delirious at the prospect.

This woman will be mine.

"My dear Lady Clementine," trilled a female voice from the hall. "It is Lady Featherstone."

Clementine's eyes went wide as they met his. "Lady

Featherstone?" she squeaked, alarm in her voice. "What could she possibly want?"

"I've no inkling." And moreover, he was damned nettled that the marchioness had chosen to arrive in a most inopportune moment, when he'd been thoroughly kissing his future bride.

The lady in question was a notorious gossip and stickler for propriety. A veritable dragon largely feared for her ability to mow down anyone in her path with so much as a word or a disapproving look.

Clementine cleared her throat. Little Fergus blinked from her lap, then came to an alert state quickly, stretching before leaping to the Axminster and scampering away to hide beneath a table.

"What shall we do?" Clementine whispered. "She can't see you here in my chamber!"

"We have just decided to remain betrothed, have we not?" he pointed out, careful to keep his voice hushed as well.

"Yes," she hissed, "but that does not mean we ought to be found here alone. That would be scandalous."

"You look thoroughly kissed," he said, and not without a bit of smugness, for he was proud of that.

He wanted to kiss her more, in fact.

He had only just begun.

He planned to kiss her everywhere. To lick her everywhere, too.

"Oh dear." She frowned.

Knock, knock, knock. "Lady Clementine?"

"You have to answer her," he said. "She doesn't sound as if she intends to go away otherwise."

He could not contain his grin. Yes, he was ridiculously happy. Far too happy for a man about to be caught by a dragon marchioness in a scandalous situation.

Although, in fairness, this was the most well-behaved he

had been in a lady's presence in as long as he could recall. He had earned his reputation by playing the rogue well and often. By the old Ambrose's standards, being alone with a lady who remained fully clothed whilst a bed was a dozen steps away was bloody miraculous.

Someone ought to award him a medal.

"How can you be grinning at a moment like this?" his betrothed groused.

"Because I'm happy." He was still grinning.

Indeed, he doubted it was physically possible to keep the smile from his face just now. Not even the impending doom of being discovered alone with Clementine by a termagant like Lady Featherstone was enough to do it.

"But this is terrible."

"It is rather reminiscent of the times *you* found couples alone, is it not?" he could not resist asking.

Knock, knock, knock. "I know you're within, my dear. I'm afraid it's a rather urgent matter."

"Answer her," he said.

"Just a moment, Lady Featherstone," she called.

"Go to the door," he directed, not certain of how this drama of theirs would play out but knowing they needed to see it to the fall of the curtain.

Clementine's eyes widened. "Where shall you go?"

"Out this window?" he suggested, having no intention of attempting such an escape.

They were on the third bloody floor of the manor house, nary a nearby tree upon whose facilitating branches he could find purchase. The drop was—he glanced down—of the broken neck variety.

"It's too high," Clementine protested.

Concern for him—a sign most excellent. His grin deepened.

"You are still grinning," she accused.

"I can't seem to stop it." He shrugged, unapologetic.

Something had overtaken him—a calming, deep sense of peace. For the first time in as long as he could remember, everything felt utterly and completely right. There was no other way to describe it, save one word.

Love.

"You must hide under the bed," Clementine said.

He glanced in the direction of the walnut tester in question. "Here now, darling. I'm not a cat."

The only sign of Fergus was his tiny orange tail, peeking from beneath the table.

"You shall fit," she determined and then shoved him in the direction of the furniture.

More knocks ensued.

On a heavy sigh, Ambrose decided to oblige his betrothed. He crossed the room, lowered himself to the thick woolen carpets, and slid beneath the bed. From his vantage place, he watched the sweep of Clementine's hem, her feet stocking-clad.

His cock became inconveniently hard at the sight of those silk stockings, for they were crimson, and they outlined the dainty turn of her ankle to perfection. Damnation, this would not do. Clementine's skirts were to his right now, gliding elegantly over the floor. She stopped at the door, and the sound of it opening resonated in the quiet of the room.

"Forgive me," Clementine was saying. "Fergus had quite a fright."

"Fergus?" The black silk skirts of the marchioness came into view as she entered the chamber. "And who is *he*, Lady Clementine?"

"Fergus is the kitten Lord Dorset rescued," Clementine answered, her skirts coming nearer once more. "We...*I* named him."

He wondered if Lady Featherstone, who was sharper than a rapier, would take note of her slip.

"You named him with the Marquess of Dorset?" the marchioness asked, not disappointing him with his opinion of her.

Clementine's ankles were once more before him, and when she moved, he caught an equally mouthwatering glimpse of her calves. Ambrose shifted to try to ease his discomfort and promptly found his face in the midst of a spider web. He made a sound of displeasure and then instantly wished to rescind the noise.

He held still, hoping no one would have heard.

"What was that sound?" Lady Featherstone queried, the black skirts coming nearer to the bed.

Blast.

The spider web on his nose began to tickle.

He was going to sneeze.

No, no, no, you dolt. Do not sneeze. Do not sneeze. Think of anything. Count to one hundred in Latin. Better yet, count backward. Centum—

The sneeze rocked through him, though he did his utmost to squelch it. The result was an emergent sound somewhere between a cough, a snort, and a grunt.

"Was that the kitten?" Lady Featherstone queried next, sounding suspicious and perplexed all at once.

Clementine coughed. "Forgive me, Lady Featherstone. It was me, I'm afraid. There was a bit of dust in my throat."

"Coughing is the act of peasants," the marchioness gently chided. "Not ladies gently bred and born."

He nearly snorted at that and wondered what Lady Featherstone thought of breaking wind.

"Of course. Pray forgive me, my lady. I'm rather at sixes and sevens today." Clementine moved once more, providing Dorset with a clear view of her tempting ankles.

When Lady Featherstone left, he was going to caress every inch of her and take his time. He was going to kiss his way from her instep all the way to her mouth. He would stop at her knees. She had lovely knees. Then kiss his way along her inner thigh. Her skin was as smooth and soft as silk there.

He suppressed another groan as a bolt of desire lanced him.

This was not helping matters.

He had to think of something else.

Anything else.

His cock was desperately, despicably hard.

"I was wondering if we might speak candidly for a few moments, my dear," Lady Featherstone was saying to Clementine. "It has come to my attention that you've begun a friendship with my daughter."

"Lady Edith is lovely," Clementine said earnestly.

"Might you know where she's gone this afternoon?" the marchioness asked.

"When we parted, she said she intended to nap in her chamber."

Lady Featherstone sighed heavily. "She's not within. I've already looked."

"Oh dear." Clementine's hem raised, her skirts swishing in agitation, and he imagined her to be clasping handfuls in her distress. "Have you checked in the library?"

"Yes."

"Have you inquired with the Duchess of Bradford?" Clementine asked next.

"I'm afraid so," Lady Featherstone said, her tone grim. "She hasn't any inkling of where Lady Edith has gone either. It's most unlike her. I greatly fear this is the influence of the Lady's Suffrage Society at work. Women are not, as you know, Lady Clementine, meant to be the equals of men."

As it turned out, listening to the marchioness speak was just the thing to make his cock shrivel. Well, at least there was a measure of reprieve to be had after all.

Clementine made a noncommittal hum, and he knew she was holding her tongue mightily. "If I see Lady Edith, I'll be sure to let her know you've been searching for her, my lady."

A clever dismissal if he'd ever heard one. And little wonder Lady Edith had fled her dragon of a mama.

Fergus chose that moment to dart from his hiding place under the table and join Dorset under the bed. The fluff of orange sidled up to his face, leaving him with not just dust and cobwebs to contend with but fur as well.

Do not sneeze again, he warned himself.

Centum, nonaginta novem, nonaginta et octo...

This time, he bit his lip and held his breath, barely suppressing the sneeze. As his body jerked with the effort to subdue it, he frightened Fergus, who hissed and went racing away.

"What in heaven's name could have disturbed the poor kitten so under that bed?" Lady Featherstone asked suspiciously.

He began to pray that he would not suffer the disgrace of being caught beneath Clementine's bed by the gossiping marchioness. *Not today, Lord.*

"Perhaps he saw a spider," Clementine suggested brightly, stepping between Lady Featherstone and the end of the bed.

"Hmm," the marchioness said, as if she did not quite believe the explanation. "Perhaps. I shall send a chambermaid to you soon to see that the area under your bed is tidied. In, shall we say, ten minutes, Lady Clementine? And in return, I trust that you'll keep Lady Edith's absence to yourself."

He would have laughed had his current situation not been so tenuous. Instead, he waited as Clementine declared ten minutes would be perfect and then escorted Lady Featherstone to the door.

Blast. He would have far preferred twenty.

There, Lady Featherstone paused. "I hope you know what you're about, marrying a roué like Dorset. No good shall come of it. Everyone knows rakes make the worst husbands."

He ground his molars, tempted to emerge from his hiding place and give the woman a sound dressing down. But Clementine came to his defense swiftly.

"I've no doubt his lordship will make an excellent husband," Clementine said softly, "and I can assure you, my heart is filled."

So is mine, my love. So is mine.

Dorset waited for the door to close, then counted to five before deeming it safe to emerge from his ignominious hiding place. He pulled himself from under the bed and stood, brushing the dust from his trousers. Clementine rushed to him.

Her brilliant, sky-blue eyes were wide. "Ambrose, Lady Featherstone suspects you were hiding under the bed. She has given us ten minutes before a chambermaid will arrive to clean the *spider* from beneath it."

He flashed her a wry grin, attempting to wipe the remnants of the very real cobweb from his face. "Then we shall have to use the next nine minutes most wisely, shall we not?"

"Lord Dorset," she said, smiling back at him. "You are an utter rogue."

"A roué, if Lady Featherstone is to be believed," he corrected, and not without a hint of bitterness. "Are you certain you know what you are doing with me?"

"I think I have an idea or two of what I'd like to do with you," said his beautiful, wicked girl.

He drew her into his arms, and then he took her lips with

his. How good she felt there, how right her mouth beneath his.

"I cannot bloody well wait to marry you," he murmured into their kiss.

"Same, darling," she said. "Same." She wrapped her arms around his neck, kissing him back.

He intended to make the best of his nine minutes.

And from then on, the rest of their lives.

EPILOGUE

"Perhaps I ought to check your night rail for bees, Lady Dorset."

The low timbre of Ambrose's teasing voice sent heat to her core.

His wicked grin made her want to kiss him.

He was her husband now, standing on the threshold of the door joining their chambers.

Husband.

What a wondrous word.

"I have not been wandering in a garden recently," she told him, playing the coquette. "However, I'm not wearing drawers."

His emerald gaze ran over her with hungry approval, and she felt it as surely as if he had run his long fingers over her bare skin. She was ever aware of her state, barefoot and freshly bathed, clad in nothing but a nightgown from her trousseau that had been commissioned with the explicit intent of tempting him. They had been waiting for this moment for what seemed a lifetime but had in truth been a mere two months.

Two months of waiting, longing, yearning to become husband and wife.

Of growing closer. Getting to know each other in every way they could. Kissing whenever they could chance it. And more. Ambrose had not entirely surrendered his rakish nature. Clementine could not say she minded.

"No drawers, you say?" He approached her with undisguised carnal intent.

"None," she confirmed, no longer able to remain where she was, positioned before the very old looking glass in her apartments.

Instead, she moved toward him, meeting him halfway. No more pretense. She threw herself into his arms, and he caught her, spinning her in a circle as if she were as light as a doll when she knew the opposite to be true. She clung to his broad shoulders, head tipped back, laughter spilling from her lips, joy overflowing in her heart.

This was their very first night as husband and wife. They were not the only newlyweds. Ambrose's valet and Clementine's lady's maid had recently found love and married as well. Their new household had journeyed, after their wedding—which had been attended by their families and dearest friends old and new—to Tildon Court. Here, Clementine had discovered not a draughty pile of ruins but instead a home worthy of its fanciful name.

A home they would restore to its true, shining glory together. Although Ambrose wanted her to keep her dowry, she'd refused. It would be put to far better use for their home and their future family.

For now, she had felt nary a draught. Nor had she spied a mouse. The furnishings were elegant and sturdy, the castle itself rich in history and family relics. Complete with newly discovered Roman ruins. It was Clementine's fondest wish that all her friends would join them here for visits. The ruins would prove an excellent lure for Lady Edith. The rest…well, Clementine had no doubt they would visit as well.

"We ought to host a house party," she said, seizing upon the same idea as Vivi.

Ambrose buried his face in her throat, kissing her where her heart was beating so wildly, she feared it might leap from her skin and gallop away. "Mmm. To the devil with house parties."

Her feet were still dangling above the thick, woolen carpets. Giddiness descended as his wicked mouth trailed a path of sin along her neck. "I was thinking we might host one of our own here at Tildon Court. Next summer, perhaps, after we have had the chance to restore the east wing's roof…"

Her words trailed off as his mouth opened over her skin, sucking.

"Oh," she said then, more moan than intelligent addition to the sentence she had never completed.

But how could she be blamed? Her husband was a handsome rogue, and he was waging war upon her senses and mind both.

He bit the cord of her neck gently. "Yes. No talk of house parties just yet. The night is ours, and I intend to enjoy it—and you—to the fullest."

He settled her on her feet, but she didn't remove her arms from around his neck. Instead, she remained as she was, body pressed to his, the thinnest scrap of linen and the rich silk of his dressing gown the only barriers between them. He was rigid, stiff and thick against her, pressing into her belly.

Feeling bold now, she reached between them to caress his length. "How shall you enjoy me?"

Her husband was nothing like Walter had been. He was not a heartless rake, not an inconstant scoundrel, and he loved her endlessly. He made her happy. He had taught her that together, they could revel in their connection and bring each other to the heights of satisfaction.

"Careful, Lady Dorset," he said, even as he thrust against her seeking hand. "If you drive me too wild, this night will be over before it has begun."

She stroked him, ignoring his warning in favor of the rush of power she felt whenever she was able to make this tall, strong man go weak for her. It was frightfully easier than she had ever imagined.

"Shall I stop?" she asked—her hand stilling—already knowing the answer.

"Christ, no," he growled, the sound low and lusty. "Open my dressing gown. I want your bare hand on my cock."

His raw words, steeped in longing, landed between her thighs, where she pulsed and ached. She was already wet and ready for him.

"Ask nicely, my lord," she said, giving him another caress and circling the broad tip with her thumb.

She wondered if a pearled drop of his mettle was leaking there.

"Please," he gritted when she continued teasing him.

She sought his mouth, kissing him deeply as she released her hold on his cock and found the knot on his dressing gown instead. As their mouths moved in unison, the kiss deepening, she tugged at the belt, and the robe parted, gaping open. The heat of his bare skin was a welcome warmth radiating into her own body. Her fingers encircled him.

He groaned into their kiss before breaking it and looking down at her, a beautiful man filled with love and drunk on pleasure. "Damn it, darling, you're not being fair."

"Am I not?" She clasped him as she knew he liked and stroked once, twice, thrice. He was thickening. Growing larger. Longer.

"I taught you too bloody much," he growled.

"We shall see," she returned teasingly, before dropping to her knees. She glanced up at him, admiring every bit of his strong, masculine body on display for her, and met his eyes. "I love you, Ambrose."

Then, she took him into her mouth.

~

HIS WIFE KNEW what he liked. And she was using it against him. He couldn't lie. He loved it. He loved *her*. And now, she was his in truth. No more bloody furtive meetings attempting to keep from her mother's hawkish eye and no more zealous gossiping marchionesses to keep them apart. No more waiting. They were husband and wife, inextricably bound.

Clementine's perfectly formed lips parted. She was on her knees before him. He ought to protest. Tell her to stop, to wait. But...those lips were on his cock now, moving, gliding. She took him deep into the hot, velvety recesses of her mouth. Sucked. Swirled her tongue over his cock head. Grasped his ballocks with enough pressure to make him lose his restraint.

But no. This was not the way their wedding night would proceed. If it did, he would be a dreadful disappointment to his bride.

Every part of his body screamed in protest as he tenderly disengaged from her before he spent in her mouth. Her lips were parted, full and swollen and glistening in the dim oil lamps. There was no electricity here at Tildon Court, which meant they relied on lamp and candle to illuminate the darkest recesses of the castle. It was slightly medieval, as was the sight of his woman on the carpets before him, intent upon giving him pleasure.

He liked that about Clementine—she was sure of herself.

Actually, he liked *everything* about her. Loved every part of her.

He took her hands in his before she could protest, tugging her to her feet even as his cock stood painfully erect between them. He felt a bit foolish as he stood there half nude, his prick glistening with her saliva and standing at attention. But she easily quelled the emotion by grasping handfuls of her night rail and raising it over her head.

The wispy garment was tossed beyond her shoulder and landed somewhere. He knew not where. Nor did he give a good goddamn. Because his wife was naked before him, all cream and the sweet, delicate pink of a rosebud. Generous curves and dips and silken, womanly flesh.

He had no words.

All he could do was take her in his arms once more and carry her to the bed awaiting them. His feet moved. His body and his mind were one as he laid Clementine on the turned-down bedclothes. The sweet scent of her teased him. Spurred him on.

He joined her, their bodies aligning, her thighs opening to invite him.

"I love you, Clementine," he said, searching for her lips.

"I love you," she answered.

And then, the time for talking was distinctly at an end. He kissed her mouth but needed more. Needed her writhing and crying out beneath him. Down her neck, he went, dragging his lips, offering kisses and sucks and licks and nips.

Her breasts were twin handfuls, creamy and ripe. He leveraged himself on one elbow while he took his time caressing them, weighing them in his hands, lowering his head to suck her nipples until her back arched and her fingers were sifting through his hair.

Lower.

Down her belly.

He found a particularly entrancing patch of skin on her hip, where her curves put Venus to shame. Everywhere, she was sweet-scented and gorgeous and far more than he deserved. At last, when she was writhing beneath him, he lowered himself between her legs. Planted his palms on her inner thighs and spread her wide.

Pink, glistening lips and a swollen bud hidden in the thatch of dark curls beckoned him. He sucked her clitoris first. Used his tongue to stroke and tease until her breaths were coming heavy and hard and her hips were undulating beneath him, and her fingers were tugging in his hair and the sweetest noises of frustration escaped her.

"Oh, Ambrose. More, please. Harder, faster," she begged.

He obliged.

Licking, sucking. He plunged his tongue into her cunny, then drew on her pearl until she cried out and the glide of his fingers in her tight passage had her coming undone for the first time.

When he could not prolong the pleasure a moment more, he rose over her, his fingers strumming her clitoris as she arched into him.

Dorset kissed her cheek, her ear, as he rolled his hips against hers. "Are you ready, my love?"

"I have been ready for you forever," she said, her fingernails raking down his back lightly, pressing her breasts into his chest.

That was all the encouragement he needed. He braced himself on one arm and grasped his aching cock in the other, bringing himself to her dripping entrance. She was so wet. So inviting. So hot.

His hips jerked, his body telling him he needed to be inside this woman. That he had been waiting to be inside this woman for his entire life. He moved, the tip of his cock inside her.

She was so tight. She relaxed beneath him on a sigh.

Heaven.

He stilled. "How does it feel, darling?"

"Perfectly wonderful." She smiled up at him, a blend of sweetness and raw eroticism that had him groaning. "I want more of you, Ambrose."

He would give her more. He would give her everything.

Slowly, he moved. Deeper. Her slick sheath welcomed him as her hips rose from the bed, urging him on. He settled his mouth over hers, sealing their lips in a tender kiss as he thrust, filling her.

She made a soft sound of need that undid him. He held himself still for as long as he could, savoring this moment of complete joining between them, memorizing her lips beneath his, her body sweetly yielding, her breasts full and round against his chest, her cunny gripping him as if, instinctively, she never wanted to let him go. How he wished he might stay here, as close to her as he could be, forever.

But his body reminded him that was impossible. Desire roared. This was what he had been waiting for, all bloody summer long. Clementine as his wife. Claiming her. Making love to her until they were both mindless and breathless.

He withdrew almost completely, the slide of his cock in her enough to fill him with a conflagration of desire and fire. Of love and need. Desperate need. Another sound tore from her. A moan this time. And he thrust to the hilt. *God*, it was good. So bloody good. Better somehow, now that she was his in every way.

He reached between them to where their bodies connected to tease the plump bud peeking from her folds. She cried out, tightening on him. Mindless. He had no more capacity for thought. He slid in and out, his fingers strumming over her pearl, his lips feasting on hers. Everything around him was a kaleidoscope of sensation: the lushness of her curves, the musky scent of her desire mingling with jasmine, the soft glow of the oil lamp illuminating them in an otherworldly glow.

They became more frenzied, clutching each other, moving together, both of them ravenous for each other. Love for her rose, poignant and fierce in his chest. For as long as he lived, he would never forget this night, this moment.

Deeper, faster.

She tightened on him, crying out as she reached her crescendo. *Ah.* He couldn't resist much longer, regardless of how desperately he wanted to prolong their lovemaking. Two more thrusts, and he broke their kiss to throw back his head as he spilled inside her.

For a moment, he collapsed, drained and awed from the ferocity of their joining. His heart pounded furiously, his breathing was raw and ragged, and he was more sated than he ever recalled being.

Clementine clutched him to her, hands gently stroking down his back, her face pressed to the top of his head, the warm reassurance of her breath ruffling his hair. They were silent, hearts beating in harmony, bodies entwined.

"I love you so much," she murmured into the silence that had descended, her fingertips gliding over his spine in a tender caress.

He pressed a kiss to the curve of her breast and then raised his head, falling into her sky-blue eyes. "And I love you. More than I ever could have imagined possible."

They shared a smile, and he reached up to smooth a tendril of hair from her cheek. He wanted to give her anything she wanted, to make her happy, to fill her life with love and laughter, to make amends for her every heartache and disappointment. He was a besotted fool, it was true. Words rose, feelings, sentiments, but his wife was quicker than he.

"Ambrose?" she asked softly, those knowing fingers trailing fire over his shoulders now.

He was utterly infatuated. This beautiful woman had ruined him for life, and he knew nary a regret.

"Yes, my love?"

"I do believe I heard buzzing. Do you think you might check to make certain there is no bee after all?" A wicked gleam had entered her gaze.

One he recognized and approved of most emphatically.

"Already?"

She nodded, moving suggestively beneath him. "Do you mind?"

He was already growing hard. "Of course not, darling. I'm yours to command."

And then he made his way down her luscious body to prove it.

~

THANK you for reading Ambrose and Clementine's story! I hope that you adored this happily ever after between a determined matchmaker and her reluctant fake fiancé and that you're eager to see what will happen as the house party continues to unfold. Lady Edith and the mysterious Mr. Valentine Blakemoor are up next, and if you like revenge, enemies-to-lovers, a bluestocking heroine who comes out of her shell in a big way, and a sinful rake who's about to be reformed, do read on for a sneak peek or grab your copy of *Forever Her Rake* here.

Please stay in touch! The only way to be sure you'll know what's next from me is to sign up for my newsletter here: http://eepurl.com/dyJSar. Please join my reader group for early excerpts, cover reveals, and more here: https://www.facebook.com/groups/scarlettscottreaders. And if you're in the mood to chat all things steamy historical romance and read a different book together each month, join my book club, Dukes Do It Hotter right here: https://www.facebook.com/groups/hotdukes because we're having a whole lot of fun! Now, on to that sneak peek of Lady Edith and Val's HEA…

Forever Her Rake
Dukes Most Wanted
Book Three

After spending all her life pinned beneath her overbearing mother's thumb, Lady Edith Smythe is desperately weary of being a respectable, dutiful daughter. What better time to finally cast aside her wallflower ways than at a country house party where women's suffrage is the leading topic of the day? And there's no better man to exercise her freedom with than a diabolically handsome rake who's as sinful as he is irresistible.

Valentine Blakemoor, self-made property magnate and one of the wealthiest men in England, has been lured to the wilds of Yorkshire by the promise of vengeance. Seducing the bookish, bespectacled Lady Edith proves an embarrassingly easy feat. But once he has her in his bed, Val is bemused to discover Lady Edith is far more than the quiet, freckled spinster he believed. To his shock, he can't seem to get enough of her, which decidedly wasn't part of his plan.

For the first time in his storied career as a jaded rake, Val wants more than mere pleasure. In fact, he wants everything Lady Edith has to offer. But she's firm on her insistence that one night and her innocence are all she's willing to give. And when she discovers his true motives for pursuing her, nothing between them will ever be the same…

Chapter One

Lady Edith Smythe wondered if her mother would ever run out of wind.

"You know that you ought not trouble your mind with such dreadful nonsense as the supposed equality of the female sex, do you not?" *Maman* paused and then, as if anticipating Edith's acquiescent response, carried on before her daughter could interject. "Of course you do, my darling beloved. You know very well that the feeble and vulnerable mind of a lady could never begin to compare to the strong and abundantly clever intellect of her masculine counterpart."

"But *Maman*," she attempted to interject.

"Indeed," Lady Featherstone carried on quite as if she hadn't heard Edith, "you do me great credit. Although I do wish you would heed my warning about the dangers of wearing such an immodest-color gown. Furthermore, the décolletage is on the border of being risqué, and I should hate for anyone to think you forward. Although I daresay that there are a great deal of unabashed jezebels in attendance, a shocking number, in fact, given the Duchess of Bradford's standing in polite society…"

As her mother droned steadily on, it became apparent that she was in no danger of stopping. Instead, she hit her stride, bemoaning the state of the other guests in attendance.

"…to say nothing of that horrid Mr. Blakemoor. What can Her Grace have been thinking, inviting such a lowborn swine?" Lady Featherstone asked, looking as if she'd unintentionally scented something spoiled.

"Mr. Blakemoor seems rather charming," Edith offered, thinking of the dazzlingly handsome gentleman she'd been clandestinely admiring from the moment of his arrival at Sherborne Manor for the Duke and Duchess of Bradford's country house party. "I would hardly characterize him as swine-like."

It was the wrong thing to say to her mother.

Maman's eyebrows snapped together, her glare turning most ferocious. "Surely you haven't spoken to that wretched roué, have you, Edith darling?"

Alas, she hadn't.

Yet.

But Edith wisely kept that to herself.

She smiled at her mother. "Of course not, *Maman*. Why should I wish to do so? You've made your disapproval of him plain, and I wouldn't want to displease you."

"My dear daughter, you are such a boon to me." *Maman* smiled and gave Edith's cheek a pat, as if she were a young girl in short skirts rather than a lady fully grown. "I am so very proud of your dutiful nature."

Edith stifled a wince and forced a smile for her mother's benefit. "If you'll excuse me, *Maman*, I do believe I should like a restorative nap before dinner this evening."

While Edith had no intention of taking a nap, she did intend to go for a walk and investigate the Roman ruins. Her mother wouldn't approve of gadding about by herself, which necessitated the lie.

"An excellent notion, dearest," her mother said, beaming at her. "I shall do the same."

Another pat and her mother rose to take her leave from Edith's guest chamber. She accompanied the marchioness to the door, smiling sweetly and hoping *Maman* took a nice, long nap. Long enough that she could discreetly escape from the manor house and take some fresh air.

Edith watched her mother disappear down the hall and then into her own room, breathing a sigh of relief as the door snapped closed on the marchioness's black silk skirts.

Freedom.

Even if only for the next hour, all the time she dared to seize for herself. Hastily, she returned to her chamber and changed into a pair of stout boots and a simple walking gown, all the better to navigate the uneven fields on her way to the ruins. Fortune was smiling upon her, for she made it through the manor house without running across any fellow guests. She slipped out a side door leading to the gardens, tying the ribbon of her jaunty hat to keep it in place.

Edith had carefully planned this little adventure. She knew the quickest means of getting to the ruins was to proceed through the boxwood maze and then via a copse of wizened old oaks. Excitement soared through her as she traversed the gravel path of the maze on her way to the ruins at last. She'd been waiting to explore ever since their arrival at Sherborne Manor several days before, and she'd begun to fear she would never be able to escape *Maman*'s observant eye.

Now, she was at last able to—

Edith's wildly racing thoughts died when she rounded a corner in the maze and collided with someone. A very hard, very tall, very well-muscled someone. A *gentleman* someone. Hands spanned her waist in a protective grasp, keeping her from an ignominious tumble to the gravel.

"Going somewhere, Lady Edith?" drawled a deep, darkly amused masculine voice.

Heart pounding, Edith stared up at the wickedly handsome face of none other than the recent topic of conversation between herself and *Maman*.

Mr. Valentine Blakemoor.

His eyes were a bright blue to rival the sky beyond, and beneath his hat, his dark hair possessed dashing, devil-may-care waves that made her stubborn fingers itch to trace them. His chiseled cheekbones and jaw were angular, the latter covered in a dark stubble that made him appear almost dangerous. And if his reputation was to be believed, he was indeed perilous—to one's virtue, that was. Little wonder. Mr. Blakemoor's mouth itself was a sin, his lips full and sensual, the sort of beautiful temptation that made her wonder what it would feel like on hers.

Wonderful, she was sure.

"Lady Edith?" he prodded, frowning down at her. "Are you injured?"

He knew her name. They hadn't been formally introduced; her mother had patently refused any association with him. But how absurd. Handsome rakes with leonine elegance and silver tongues such as Mr. Blakemoor didn't notice plain, red-haired spinsters with spectacles and far too many freckles.

She blinked, terribly aware of his hands on her, of his body's nearness to hers. "I am…quite well," she managed to say, with only a hint of breathlessness stealing into her words.

Except she wasn't well. She was hot all over. Mr. Blakemoor was even more handsome at this reckless proximity than he was from afar.

"Excellent," he said, giving her a slow grin that made something inside her melt. "I wouldn't wish to do you harm."

How could such simple, felicitous words feel intimate, as if he were suggesting something iniquitous? Her cheeks felt as if they were baking beneath the blaze of a summer sun.

"Chivalrous of you," she said, thinking that she wanted him to release her at once.

Also, she never wanted him to let go.

She wanted to bask in the glory of his masculine perfection. To be the sole recipient of his intense regard.

His lips curved higher, revealing dimples that bracketed that sinner's mouth of his. "My dear Lady Edith, I do hate to disappoint you, but I haven't a chivalrous bone in my body."

Warmth pooled in her belly at those words. It was silly, she knew. He wasn't flirting with her. Why would he? She was a bookish wallflower. He could have his pick of any of the ladies in London.

She cleared her throat, feeling foolish. "Thank you for the warning, sir. If you'll excuse me, I must be on my way. I haven't much time before my mother wakes from her nap."

"Ah, the dragon sleeps," he said, still not releasing her. "Where are you going, my lady?"

"For a walk to see the Roman ruins," she answered before she could think better of it.

"Allow me to escort you," he said smoothly, releasing her and taking a step back as if he were indeed the perfect gentleman he claimed not to be. "I insist."

She opened her mouth to tell him no. That under no circumstances would she dare to allow him to escort her to the Roman ruins. *Alone.* But then her inner rebel took the reins, and she thought of how horrified *Maman* would be if she discovered Edith had been unchaperoned with Mr. Blakemoor.

And she smiled. "How kind of you to offer. I'd be happy for the company."

Want more? Get *Forever Her Rake*!

DON'T MISS SCARLETT'S OTHER ROMANCES!

Complete Book List
HISTORICAL ROMANCE

Heart's Temptation
A Mad Passion (Book One)
Rebel Love (Book Two)
Reckless Need (Book Three)
Sweet Scandal (Book Four)
Restless Rake (Book Five)
Darling Duke (Book Six)
The Night Before Scandal (Book Seven)

Wicked Husbands
Her Errant Earl (Book One)
Her Lovestruck Lord (Book Two)
Her Reformed Rake (Book Three)
Her Deceptive Duke (Book Four)
Her Missing Marquess (Book Five)
Her Virtuous Viscount (Book Six)

DON'T MISS SCARLETT'S OTHER ROMANCES!

League of Dukes
Nobody's Duke (Book One)
Heartless Duke (Book Two)
Dangerous Duke (Book Three)
Shameless Duke (Book Four)
Scandalous Duke (Book Five)
Fearless Duke (Book Six)

Notorious Ladies of London
Lady Ruthless (Book One)
Lady Wallflower (Book Two)
Lady Reckless (Book Three)
Lady Wicked (Book Four)
Lady Lawless (Book Five)
Lady Brazen (Book 6)

Unexpected Lords
The Detective Duke (Book One)
The Playboy Peer (Book Two)
The Millionaire Marquess (Book Three)
The Goodbye Governess (Book Four)

Dukes Most Wanted
Forever Her Duke (Book One)
Forever Her Marquess (Book Two)
Forever Her Rake (Book Three)

The Wicked Winters
Wicked in Winter (Book One)
Wedded in Winter (Book Two)
Wanton in Winter (Book Three)
Wishes in Winter (Book 3.5)
Willful in Winter (Book Four)
Wagered in Winter (Book Five)

DON'T MISS SCARLETT'S OTHER ROMANCES!

Wild in Winter (Book Six)
Wooed in Winter (Book Seven)
Winter's Wallflower (Book Eight)
Winter's Woman (Book Nine)
Winter's Whispers (Book Ten)
Winter's Waltz (Book Eleven)
Winter's Widow (Book Twelve)
Winter's Warrior (Book Thirteen)
A Merry Wicked Winter (Book Fourteen)

The Sinful Suttons
Sutton's Spinster (Book One)
Sutton's Sins (Book Two)
Sutton's Surrender (Book Three)
Sutton's Seduction (Book Four)
Sutton's Scoundrel (Book Five)
Sutton's Scandal (Book Six)
Sutton's Secrets (Book Seven)

Rogue's Guild
Her Ruthless Duke (Book One)
Her Dangerous Beast (Book Two)
Her Wicked Rogue (Book 3)

Royals and Renegades
How to Love a Dangerous Rogue (Book One)

Sins and Scoundrels
Duke of Depravity
Prince of Persuasion
Marquess of Mayhem
Sarah
Earl of Every Sin
Duke of Debauchery

DON'T MISS SCARLETT'S OTHER ROMANCES!

Viscount of Villainy

Sins and Scoundrels Box Set Collections
Volume 1
Volume 2

The Wicked Winters Box Set Collections
Collection 1
Collection 2
Collection 3
Collection 4

Wicked Husbands Box Set Collections
Volume 1
Volume 2

Stand-alone Novella
Lord of Pirates

CONTEMPORARY ROMANCE
Love's Second Chance
Reprieve (Book One)
Perfect Persuasion (Book Two)
Win My Love (Book Three)

Coastal Heat
Loved Up (Book One)

ABOUT THE AUTHOR

USA Today and Amazon bestselling author Scarlett Scott writes steamy Victorian and Regency romance with strong, intelligent heroines and sexy alpha heroes. She lives in Pennsylvania and Maryland with her Canadian husband, their adorable identical twins, two sweet dogs, and one zany cat.

A self-professed literary junkie and nerd, she loves reading anything, but especially romance novels, poetry, and Middle English verse. Catch up with her on her website https://scarlettscottauthor.com. Hearing from readers never fails to make her day.

Scarlett's complete book list and information about upcoming releases can be found at https://scarlettscottauthor.com.

Connect with Scarlett! You can find her here:
Join Scarlett Scott's reader group on Facebook for early excerpts, giveaways, and a whole lot of fun!
Sign up for her newsletter here
https://www.tiktok.com/@authorscarlettscott

- facebook.com/AuthorScarlettScott
- x.com/scarscoromance
- instagram.com/scarlettscottauthor
- bookbub.com/authors/scarlett-scott
- amazon.com/Scarlett-Scott/e/B004NW8N2I
- pinterest.com/scarlettscott

Printed in Great Britain
by Amazon